Samuel French Acting Edition

Scapino

by Jeffrey Binder

For all enquiries regarding motion picture, television, and other media rights, please contact Concord Theatricals.

MUSIC USE NOTE

Licensees are solely responsible for obtaining formal written permission from copyright owners to use copyrighted music in the performance of this play and are strongly cautioned to do so. If no such permission is obtained by the licensee, then the licensee must use only original music that the licensee owns and controls. Licensees are solely responsible and liable for all music clearances and shall indemnify the copyright owners of the play(s) and their licensing agent, Concord Theatricals, against any costs, expenses, losses and liabilities arising from the use of music by licensees. Please contact the appropriate music licensing authority in your territory for the rights to any incidental music.

IMPORTANT BILLING AND CREDIT REQUIREMENTS

If you have obtained performance rights to this title, please refer to your licensing agreement for important billing and credit requirements.

SCAPINO first opened on February 17, 2018 at Gulfshore Playhouse (Founding and Producing Artistic Director, Kristen Coury) in Naples, Florida. The production was directed by Zeljko Djukic, with scenic design by Kurtis Boetcher, costume design by Natasha V. Djukic, lighting design by Jimmy Lawlor, and sound design by Jeffrey Levin. The production stage manager was Emily Hauger. The cast was as follows:

OCTAVIO	Jack Berenholtz
SYLVESTER	Phillip Taratula
SCAPINO	Jeffrey Binder
CHLOE	Monica Rae Summers Gonzalez
DON ALBERT	Gerritt VanderMeer
DON JERRY GERONTE	Larry Paulsen
LEO	Grayson Powell
FEATHER	Jade Radford

Special Thanks

Kristen Coury, Zeljko and Natasha Djukic, Andrew Paul, David Whalen, Wesley Mann, Morgan Snowden, Jack Lafferty, Ethan Saks, Sarah Silk, Kevin McConville, Elijah Conley, Cam Nickel, Melissa Hill Grande, Angela Baughman, Johnmichael Bohach, Kim Brown, Alex Stevens, Rachel Ferrari Engel, Joniece Abbot-Pratt, Alex Mandell, Danny Rutigliano, Daniel Everidge, Timothy Carter, Lindsay Warnick, Jonathan "Yogurty Goodness" Binder, Farrell Binder, Indigo Ocean, Annette and Joe Anderson, Cory Dunn, Patty and Jay Baker, Allen and Joyce Gerstein, Pete Zepeda, and Pete Zepeda.

CHARACTERS

SCAPINO – A con artist and a trickster. Also a lawyer.

SYLVESTER – Scapino's anxious sidekick but Octavio's number two.

DON JERRY GERONTE (pronounced GERONT-EE) – The brutal, bull-headed, skinflint boss of one of the most notorious crime families in Naples.

DON ALBERT – The brutal, calculating, coiffed boss of one of the other most notorious crime families in Naples.

OCTAVIO – Don Albert's handsome, devoted, very emotional and self-obsessed son. In love with Chloe.

CHLOE – The beautiful, devoted, very emotional and driven secret wife of Octavio.

LEO – Don Geronte's large and dangerous son. Also devoted puppy dog in love with Feather.

FEATHER – A free spirit. The fiery and socially aware lover of Leo.

Note: In terms of non-traditional casting, please cast this show freely and funnily.

SETTING

The dangerous streets of luxurious Naples, Florida on a day like this one...only even *more* dangerous.

PACING

Scapino should be performed at the speed of fun.

AUTHOR'S NOTES

Scapino embraces an old commedia style, but delivers it in a fully modern way – please feel free to replace or update topical references as noted, change Chicago to a more relevant city that will connect more with your local audience, or otherwise embrace the unique timing of found lazzis to bring a fresh, contemporary sensibility to the humor. Make the jokes your own.

What makes or breaks *Scapino* is Scapino's relationship with the audience. The character Scapino in particular should feel free to look at them, smile at them, toss lines to them, wink and nod at them, seduce them, and otherwise break the fourth wall with comic impunity to enlist them into his or her machinations and make them feel as though they're part of the scheming and "in on the joke." Exploring that interplay with the audience will only help heighten the comedy in performance.

It's equally important to find and land those moments when the play becomes deadly serious – don't shy away from pulling the rug out from under the audience mid-laugh. Keep them guessing and off-balance. It's a comedy, but the undercurrent of love, fury, need, violence, and betrayal keeps the stakes high and the ball in the air as much as the fun. Don't lose sight of the fact that this is a dangerous game they're all playing – the cost of failure (for all of them) is catastrophic. And hilarious.

To my dad, Joseph Binder, who taught me humor. To my mom, Gail Binder, who taught me heart. To my daughter, Annika Jae Anderson-Binder, who taught me the lengths you will go for family. To my husband, Michael Anderson, who taught me everything else (and helped make every bit of this script better). I love all you all more than words.

And, of course, to Molière – the genius who came up with the idea in the first place.

ACT ONE

Scene One

*(**OCTAVIO** enters in a panic.)*

OCTAVIO. *(To audience.)* Oh, God. This is terrible news. Awful. I can't breathe. I think I'm having a panic attack. I'm too sensitive for this.

*(**SYLVESTER** enters. He is also in a panic.)*

SYLVESTER. There you are, Octavio! We're dead men!

OCTAVIO. Ah Sylvester, my trusty man-servant.

SYLVESTER. Personal assistant.

OCTAVIO. Tell me this isn't happening Sylvester! Tell me this is all a dream – a nightmare. Tell me! Wait, don't tell me. No, tell me! Are you sure you heard it right?

SYLVESTER. Oh, I heard it right, all right! Your father's gonna break our kneecaps when he finds out.

OCTAVIO. You say Pop left a message that he's coming home?

SYLVESTER. Home, yes!

OCTAVIO. This morning?

SYLVESTER. This morning, yep.

OCTAVIO. And the only reason he's coming home early is to marry me off?

SYLVESTER. That's right.

OCTAVIO. To Don Jerry Geronte's long-lost daughter?

SYLVESTER. His daughter!

OCTAVIO. Never met her.

SYLVESTER. She's been on the lam for her own protection.

OCTAVIO. And it'll stop the turf war that's about to go nuclear between our two families?

SYLVESTER. Yeah, it'll stop it cold. Otherwise ground zero. Kerplow! Right here!

OCTAVIO. And this mystery girl... Don Jerry's bringing her out of hiding to marry me?

SYLVESTER. This very day!

OCTAVIO. Uncle Vinny delivered this message?

SYLVESTER. Uncle Vinny, yeah.

OCTAVIO. And Uncle Vinny knows everything we've been up to?

SYLVESTER. Everything *you've* been up to.

OCTAVIO. And he told my pop the whole kit-and-caboodle?

SYLVESTER. Kit? Meet caboodle! Yes!

OCTAVIO. STOP repeating everything I'm saying! You got nothing to add?

SYLVESTER. Sorry, boss. But what can I say? You're telling it exactly like it is. Which is exactly what I told you three times already!

OCTAVIO. Well help me out here! Give me some support. A shoulder to cry on! Can't you at least try to make me feel a little better about all this?

SYLVESTER. This is worse for me than it is for you, boss. Who's gonna make me feel better about it?

OCTAVIO. This news is killing me.

SYLVESTER. It's gonna kill us both!

OCTAVIO. When Pa comes back he's gonna break over me like a thunderstorm.

SYLVESTER. I'm the one who promised to keep you out of trouble. Don Albert's gonna storm all right. It's gonna be a hailstorm. Like a hailstorm of blows from a baseball bat all over my head, my hands, my kneecaps. Like my teeth falling like rain from the downpour of his brass-knuckled fist. Like a rainbow of –

OCTAVIO. All right, I get it! Enough with the storm metaphors. What do I do?

SYLVESTER. You don't care what happens to me at all, do you?

OCTAVIO. Of course I do, a little. You're like a brother to me, kinda. Now how do I get out of this? I'm losing it.

SYLVESTER. Maybe you should have thought of what would happen before you got us into this.

OCTAVIO. All right your holiness, enough with the sermonizing.

SYLVESTER. And enough with the getting into messes in the first place without having an exit strategy!

OCTAVIO. *(Sincerely.)* Sylvester, you're right. Oh, curse my irresistible manliness! Your reprimands are bringing me to tears. What do I do? How do you help me save myself?!

SYLVESTER. I'm helpless! We need a miracle!

Scene Two

(**SCAPINO** *enters. Miraculously.*)

SCAPINO. Gents.

SYLVESTER. Tony! Tony Scapino! Back in town! How ya been? (*Under his breath to* **SCAPINO.**) Thank God you're here. Octavio is in the dumps, and if you can't help him I'm going in the dumpster.

SCAPINO. What do you mean?

OCTAVIO. Ah, Tony. Tony, Tony, Tony…look at me. You see before you a broken man. Just put me in a box and dump me in the canals…

SCAPINO. Why? What's wrong with both of you?

OCTAVIO. You don't know?

SCAPINO. No, I just got here.

OCTAVIO. Oh, Scapino! My pop is on his way back to Naples.

SCAPINO. Don Albert? How was his trip?

OCTAVIO. Very lucrative and the weather was just beautiful. But he's been making nice with Don Jerry Geronte. Pop wants to mend the rift between families by marrying me off to Don Jerry's daughter.

SCAPINO. Oh. Is that it?

OCTAVIO. What do you mean "is that it"?

SCAPINO. As problems go it's not that…

OCTAVIO. No, you don't get it!

SCAPINO. Obviously not. It's about time you settled down. But I take it from your expression there's more to this story. And I take it I'm about to hear it.

OCTAVIO. You are.

SCAPINO. Lay it on me.

OCTAVIO. Scapino, you always did good as the family consigliere…and I've always admired you for your devious mind and your carefree sense of fashion. If you could figure out some kinda trick to slip me outta this mess I've gotten myself into, I swear on the blessed memory of my sweet mother that I will be forever in your debt and carry the bond of our friendship to the grave.

SCAPINO. Whoa. Wait. You said a trick? A hoodwink? A scheme? A gull? Well, my boy, I gotta say you've come to the master. I don't like to blow my own horn, so to speak, but I could cheat a nun out of her habit if I had a mind to do it. Half a mind. I am a wily wolf among sheep. I have a towering talent for trickery. I can twist the truth like a pretzel. I can spin a story like a plate on a stick. My mind is a labyrinth of lies, all smoke and mirrors. I'm like those dot paintings that you have to squint and look at sideways to see what the whole picture is –

SYLVESTER. I can never see those things.

OCTAVIO. Me neither.

SCAPINO. An artist, a colossus of chicanery. The Galileo of guile.

SYLVESTER. You're a lawyer.

SCAPINO. Exactly! I'm a *lawyer*. For the family. *Was* a lawyer. Truth be told, this artist has put down his brush. Ever since I got ratted out by one of our own.

OCTAVIO. What do you mean, Scapino?

SYLVESTER. Where've you been anyway?

SCAPINO. I took a hit for the family, Sylvester. I played the patsy, the fall guy...

SYLVESTER. Jeepers, Tony. The cops?

SCAPINO. Bingo, Sylvester. I had a rather unfortunate conversation with the authorities, my boys. A conversation that lasted three to five, with time off for good behavior. I've been disbarred, disgraced...diminished. So, I'm walking the straight and narrow. I've hung up my tools of the trade.

> *(He exits, leaving* **OCTAVIO** *and* **SYLVESTER** *alone in their misery. A beat.* **SCAPINO** *re-enters.)*

SCAPINO. But enough about me. You obviously want to tell me your troubles, and misery loves company, so spill the beans.

OCTAVIO. Okay, so, you know about the rift between my pop, Don Albert, and the head of the Geronte family, Don Jerry? Don't ask me how it started but it was only a matter of time before our families had to settle things fair and square, which was a real downer because Don Jerry's son Leo is my best friend and I woulda hated to whack him. But business.

SCAPINO. Got it.

OCTAVIO. So the man upstairs decided it was time to fix things between our families –

SCAPINO. The man upstairs? A miracle.

OCTAVIO. Not *that* man upstairs. Uncle Vinny. He lives in a second-floor bungalow over our garage. He's like a father to all of us.

SYLVESTER. Uncle Vinny!

SCAPINO. Uncle Vinny?

OCTAVIO. Uncle Vinny. He didn't want to have to choose sides in a turf war so he made my pop and Don Jerry yacht down to the Keys so they'd be forced to spend a lot of time together and mend fences.

SCAPINO. Got it.

OCTAVIO. We never thought our pops would do anything but kill each other once they got out onto the open water, so my best bro Leo and I decided to have one last no-holds-barred-outta-town-super-duper-party weekend before *his* pop and *my* pop got back to Naples and we had to kill each other. So of course we went to –

SCAPINO. Miami.

OCTAVIO. No, Boca Raton. Miami was all booked up.

SYLVESTER. Boca's very peaceful.

OCTAVIO. Peaceful, yes, but with a dark, seedy underbelly that comes out to play after the early bird special.

SCAPINO. Got it.

OCTAVIO. Wouldn't you know it? The first day on the beach Leo ran into this girl he'd met at some concert and fell in love. She was selling hemp bracelets.

SCAPINO. Say it ain't so.

OCTAVIO. He was, like, all crazy eyes for her, and yeah, she was all right, but I didn't think she was the knockout he thought she was. But he would not shut up about her, like all weekend. He'd talk about how smart she was, and her hair, and the cute way she would yell at him. Blah blah blah. And I was like, "Yeah, right, I get it, she's awesome, whatever," and then he's all like, "Maybe you're too stupid to understand and appreciate all her gifts," and I'm like, "Well I'm smart enough to appreciate how to unload this conceal-and-carry gift I got from Ma last Christmas, God rest her soul," and he's like –

SCAPINO. I think we're veering from the narrative a little, Octavio, let's get the exposition train back on track.

SYLVESTER. Toot toot.

OCTAVIO. Yeah, okay, right. Got it. Long story short, we had a little disagreement and I decided to stay at a youth hostile.

SYLVESTER. Hostel.

OCTAVIO. That's what I said. I decided to stay there rather than spend another night listening to Leo moon and whine over this girl. As you know Boca shuts down at 7:30 and I didn't want to break curfew –

SCAPINO. Got it.

OCTAVIO. So I'm alone in my room and staring at the ceiling and *boom* what do I hear?

SCAPINO. What?

OCTAVIO. Crying. Sobbing. But not just like annoying, shut up and get over it crying. This was transcendent. Luminous. Like the emptiness of a soulless and uncaring universe was contained in the bleat of her long, pitiful wail of despair.

SCAPINO. Her? Oh boy...

OCTAVIO. Well of course I have to find the source of this sorrow. No matter how slim the odds, no matter how long it took me, I would search out and find where this wellspring of sadness came from.

SCAPINO. And how many people were staying at this youth hostel?

OCTAVIO. Two. Including me. No one else in Boca is younger than twenty-five.

SCAPINO. Got it.

OCTAVIO. There she was, on the communal sofa – weeping, distraught. Anyone else would have looked repulsive, Scapino. Hideous. I would have spurned them. "I spurn you, puffy-faced girl." But she...oh man...she was like... her hair? Yellow and bright and fluffy like a bucket full of Twinkies. *[Alternatively: "Dark and silky and tempting like a bucket full of Ding Dongs," or the cast favorite, "Red and rich and flowing like Grandma's puttanesca...oh, Grandma..."]* And her eyes? So big and dewy and round. Moondrops and starlight. Like Bambi's eyes after the mom got all shot up in the woods.

SCAPINO. Nice.

OCTAVIO. What was I to do, Scapino? What could I do? I was smited.

SYLVESTER. Smitten.

OCTAVIO. Whatever. Put a fork in me, I was done. This girl, Scapino, *she* was that fork. She was that fork, Scapino, and I was done.

SYLVESTER. Oh, we're forked all right.

OCTAVIO. Through her tears, the puffy-faced girl told me her mother had just died suddenly, and that she had to find her father but she had no idea where he was. She was mourning not only for the mother she had lost, but for the father who had lost her.

SCAPINO. Uh-huh. And you fell in love with her.

OCTAVIO. *Whoa,* how did you know?! Yes! A heartless monster would have fallen in love with her. A werewolf!

Even Leo, when we sobered up and forgave each other and hugged like brothers, said he thought she was nice.

SCAPINO. How could he not?

OCTAVIO. I ran to her. I ran to the puffy-faced girl. I wiped her tears away with these hands, and I folded her into these arms. And as dusk dimmed into night in that crazy little village of Boca Raton, I took her back to my room at that youth hostile and I cherished her.

SCAPINO. Poetic.

SYLVESTER. OH MY GOD WE DON'T HAVE TIME FOR THIS HE'LL BE HERE ANY MINUTE! I'm sorry, let me finish this story and surprise-surprise, he's omitting a minor detail. Me. Surprise. I was there! Carrying the bags, breaking up the fights, renting the *hostile*, sleeping on the floor while he and this girl laid in bed kissing all over each other. It was so awkward! Let me give you the bottom line before we all die!

SCAPINO. I'm all ears.

SYLVESTER. Okay. So here's the skinny. He meets this crying girl, she cries, he falls in love, he can't live without her. They make out. A lot. The youth hostel lady suspects hanky-panky and threatens to bounce both of them. This girl has no money and nowhere to go. Boo hoo hoo yadda yadda yadda. Octavio throws himself at the puffy girl's feet and begs her to *marry* him.

OCTAVIO. It's true, Scapino. She has unmanned me.

SYLVESTER. Your pop is gonna unman you with scissors when he sees that ring on your finger! Anyway, she says she likes him but she's gotta think about it. She says she's gotta get to know him better. Now *he's* all boo hoo hoo yadda yadda yadda –

OCTAVIO. – Watch it. –

SYLVESTER. – But with an edge of danger –

OCTAVIO. – Thank you –

SYLVESTER. – She agrees to let him bring her back here while she thinks it over. She makes it a day before she folds like a bad hand and they *elope*. So ba da bing ba da boom. Pop is home, the families are about to go to war 'cause Octavio's let his zipper do the talking, and who do you think is gonna pay? *Staff!*

OCTAVIO. All true, Scapino. Except the zipper part. My zipper is no squealer. And Pop's gonna kill us both.

SCAPINO. Got it. And that's it? You're both such jittery Jessicas you've got *me* on edge. This is nothing. A trifle. A speedbump. And Sylvester, you're an insult to personal assistants everywhere. Look at yourself, you overgrown man-child. Coward! Why can't you scramble up some thoughts in that flaccid noodle lumped on top of your neck and figure something out. Why, I was thinking circles around these goons when I was half your age. Shame, Sylvester.

SYLVESTER. All right already! You got me, I admit it! I don't have the smarts! Mea culpa. One false move and we're all done for. So please. You gotta help us, Scapino. You're our only hope.

SCAPINO. I told you, I'm out of the...

(*We hear an ear-splitting wail.*)

OCTAVIO. Wait! Do you hear that?

(*Another wail.*)

Isn't it...the most beautiful sound you ever heard?

Scene Three

> (**CHLOE** *enters. She is distraught. And furious. And distraught-furious.*)

CHLOE. Octavio! Why?! You bastard, don't come near me! Tell me the truth. No, you don't need to tell me anything. Sylvester told me everything!

OCTAVIO. Sylvester told you?

SYLVESTER. I –

CHLOE. This is a nightmare. I can't breathe. I can't stop crying. I'm gonna drown in my own tears.

OCTAVIO. Take me with you! Let me drown with you, Chloe!

CHLOE. Hold me. No, get away from me! Oh, why did I leave Boca?!

OCTAVIO. Oh Chloe. Chloe, Chloe, Chloe. Oh my God. You know I can't take it, seeing you like this. All puffy-faced and sad.

> (*He can't take it but he's turned on.*)

I just wanna… I just wanna…

CHLOE. Wanna what, Octavio? You pig. Don't look at me that way. You monster. I don't want anything from you. I don't want your kisses, or your kissy lies.

> (*She can't take it but she's turned on.*)

I don't wanna… I don't wanna…

> (*They make out.*)

SCAPINO. This is getting out of hand.

SYLVESTER. Tell me about it.

CHLOE. (*Breaks away.*) Get away from me! I know all about your two-timing. Sylvester told me a frenemy of your father is bringing some *mystery boat girl* with him and you're gonna marry her?

OCTAVIO. Sylvester?!

SYLVESTER. I –

CHLOE. This ring on my finger for one day and you're already throwing me away? Like I'm nothing? Like I'm nobody? Take it, then! Take my ring back, if that's how you feel! You Judas! You bastard!

(*She throws the ring at* **OCTAVIO**.)

OCTAVIO. Chloe, no! How could you think that? No, baby, no! Don't throw away our bond, our golden love hoop. Look at my hand. Look, Chloe.

(*He shows her his ring on his finger.*)

Chloe, look! (*Sincerely.*) Would this still be on my finger if I was to abandon you? If I was to break my vow of eternal love? Chloe... C'mon, I love you. Lemme kiss away your heartbreak.

CHLOE. No. Yes. I dunno.

OCTAVIO. Look. I'm gonna be honest, Chloe. Though no one likes a stool pigeon, and though Sylvester will pay dearly for his loose lips –

SYLVESTER. – Forked again –

OCTAVIO. – He speaks the truth. Pop is coming and his friend and deadly rival is bringing some girl he wants to force me to marry. For the sake of the family.

(*A beat.* **CHLOE** *starts to cry.*)

Wait. Don't cry, Chloe.

(*Fighting his arousal.*) Mmmmm. Don't...oh, yeah. No. Look at me, Chloe. I would gun down a hundred Pops to keep you by my side.

CHLOE. Aw, you mean it? A hundred Pops? For me? Oh, Octavio, hold me.

(*They come together to nuzzle.*)

OCTAVIO. Aw baby, you know I would. You have my word. As a man.

CHLOE. (*Immediately pushes him away.*) Get away from me! There it is. Oh yeah, right..."as a man." Ma had a man swear to her, and then he left her and he never came back. I know all about a man's love. A woman's love is a knife, and a man's? A man's love is like butter. It melts away as soon as another knife wants a spread.

OCTAVIO. I admit that I always thought with these charms and this body, why shouldn't I spread myself around? But as soon as I saw you splayed on that sofa covered in Kleenex and...

(**CHLOE** *starts to cry.*)

For the love of all that's holy Chloe you're makin' me crazy... I just wanna... (*He resists.*) No! ...Pop will not touch your face...a face never more beautiful than it is now, wet and confused and munchable. This girl my pop wants me to marry? Already I can't stand to be near her. Just the thought of even kissing her would be like...like kissing my own sister.

CHLOE. Yeah?

OCTAVIO. Yeah.

CHLOE. Kissing your sister. Ew.

OCTAVIO. Yeah, I know, right?

CHLOE. You got a tissue? I need to dry my eyes.

OCTAVIO. Here.

(*He hands her a tissue.*)

Dry your eyes my princess. My queen. But not completely.

CHLOE. I'll leave a tear, right here. For you.

(**OCTAVIO** *puts the ring back on her finger.*)

OCTAVIO. Hot. Chloe, my love. Will you marry me? Again? Just like yesterday?

CHLOE. You're gonna make me cry again! Yes! Yes, I will. Oh, Octavio!

OCTAVIO. Oh, Chloe.

CHLOE. Oh, Oct...

(*They make out.*)

SCAPINO. These two are made for each other.

SYLVESTER. I'm a dead man.

SCAPINO. Settle down, Sylvester. Bask in the glow of young love. They'll be like us soon enough.

> *(Beat.)*

How long can they go on like this?

SYLVESTER. The record? Three hours twenty-seven minutes and forty-eight seconds.

SCAPINO. Yeesh. Okay.

> **(CHLOE** *breaks away abruptly.)*

CHLOE. No! My ears must deny your honeyed words and my mouth your silvery tongue. Be a man and fix this, Octavio! Do something!

OCTAVIO. *(On his knees.)* Scapino. I'm on my knees. This is me on my knees and I'm begging you. Help us.

CHLOE. And this is me watching him on his knees, unmanning himself before you. And I'm asking you, on behalf of my emasculated husband –

OCTAVIO. – I'm a stallion –

CHLOE. – Help us.

SYLVESTER. Please. Please, Scapino.

OCTAVIO. Pretty please.

SCAPINO. *(Considers for a moment.)* Ah, what the hell. I was never meant to grow old anyway. What's the use living if you gotta live like an accountant. No offense to accountants. All right. I'm in. I'm back in the game.

> **(OCTAVIO, CHLOE,** *and* **SYLVESTER** *celebrate.)*

Now, first things first, Octavio. You gotta welcome your father home.

OCTAVIO. Me? You know Pop – that unnerving stare, that cold smile, that icy heart. I'm the fruit of his loins and he still gives me the heebie-jeebies.

SCAPINO. Well, that's fine then. Let's just forget the whole thing. By the way, when your father finds out you've ruined his plans would you like a spade or a shovel to dig your own grave?

OCTAVIO. Point taken. What do I need to do?

SCAPINO. You must be strong, you must be firm, you must be unwavering in the face of fear! Do not hesitate! Do not falter! Use your killer instinct! Eye of the tiger. Good. Anything he throws at you, be ready to take it without a flinch, and toss it right back to him.

OCTAVIO. I'll try.

SCAPINO. No try! Do! Eye of the tiger. Show me the tiger, Octavio. Gimme a roar.

(**OCTAVIO** *roars seductively toward* **CHLOE**, *who purrs back.*)

OCTAVIO. Roar.

SCAPINO. Awwww, adorable…

(*He grabs* **OCTAVIO** *by the collar.*)

That's a pussycat! Roar, you cold-blooded killer, you! Roar like a tiger!

OCTAVIO. Roar!

SCAPINO. Better. Now. Let's do a little role-playing. I'm your pop. I'm gonna come in and I'm gonna tear you apart. You gotta stand up to me. Establish your place in the family. This is your life! Remember – Tiger, tiger, burning bright, in the forest of the –

OCTAVIO. What?!

SCAPINO. Forget it, just be mean. OKAY. I'm your pop and I'm mad. Here we go. And…SCENE!

(*He pretends to be* **OCTAVIO**'s *father.*)

You no good, ungrateful, worthless piece of dirt. You lying, knuckleheaded, stupid, moronic, nincompoop. This is how you repay me? I only ask for one thing! Respect! This is respect? You cologne-soaked, hair-coiffed, pedicured, slack-jawed, sloping-foreheaded, half-wit, rat-faced, twit-brained excuse for a two-legged insect. I oughta play *Ode to Joy* all over your face with a crowbar for what you done to me. What do you have to tell me before I tap dance all over your testicles. Well? Say something.

OCTAVIO. *(Beat.)* It's a lot like him but you're not mean enough.

SCAPINO. Octavio!

OCTAVIO. I'm sorry! But I hear those words and it reminds me of Pop and then I just shut down. Like I'm five years old again and he just found out I drank his Schlitz.

SCAPINO. That's why we're doing this! You're not five anymore. Do you want Chloe or not?

OCTAVIO. Aw man, Chloe. Like you gotta ask. Okay. You're right, Scapino. I gotta man up. Game face. Eye of the tiger. From this moment on Octavio, hitter of men, is not afraid of his father. I'm a lion. I'm a cold-hearted snake.

SCAPINO. Yeah?

OCTAVIO. Look into my eyes.

SCAPINO. Uh-oh. You ready?

OCTAVIO. Never readier.

SCAPINO. Killer instinct?

OCTAVIO. Locked and loaded.

SCAPINO. I want the truth!

OCTAVIO. You can't handle the truth!

SCAPINO. Good! 'Cause here comes your pop.

OCTAVIO. I'm out.

CHLOE. Octavio! Come back!

        (**OCTAVIO** *runs off as* **CHLOE** *runs after him.*)

SCAPINO. I think that went well.

SYLVESTER. For a colonoscopy. Nice try Scapino, but I gotta hide.

Scene Four

(**DON ALBERT** *enters, intercepting* **SYLVESTER**'s *hasty exit. Or maybe* **SYLVESTER** *tries to hide in the audience and uses a program to cover his face. In any case,* **DON ALBERT** *catches* **SYLVESTER**.)

(*He carries an ominous black bag with him.*)

DON ALBERT. Sylvester.

SYLVESTER. (*Stammering in fear.*) Don Albert!

DON ALBERT. (*To* **SYLVESTER**.) All right, you doorstop. Where is he? That rat-faced, twit-brained bum. I can hardly wait to hear his excuses, so I can rip his tongue out and feed it to him.

SCAPINO. Don Albert, so good to see you home.

DON ALBERT. Oh, hey Scapino, how's tricks?

(*To* **SYLVESTER**.) Did I not make crystal clear to you that you were to keep my idiot son out of trouble while I was gone?

SCAPINO. How was the trip?

DON ALBERT. Not bad. Very lucrative. The weather was just beautiful. Now shaddup. I appreciate your airy banter but right now I got some scores to settle.

SCAPINO. You're settling scores?

DON ALBERT. That's right.

SCAPINO. With who?

DON ALBERT. First I'm gonna smear this floor-paste here, then I'm gonna kill my son.

(*During the following, he nonchalantly pulls out various tools from the bag [hammer, drill, garden implements, etc.], evaluating the best way to torture* **SYLVESTER**. **SCAPINO** *works to distract him.*)

SCAPINO. But why?

DON ALBERT. Don't you know what's been going on while I was gone?

SCAPINO. Well, yeah, your son got married or some little thing like that...

DON ALBERT. Treason? Dishonor? Disrespect? These are little things to you?

SCAPINO. I just thought you wouldn't have cared that much about it.

DON ALBERT. Not cared? I do not understand you, Scapino. Illuminate me before I start to lose my temper.

SYLVESTER. Oh, God. He's not even mad yet, Scapino.

*(***DON ALBERT*** stuffs a gag in* **SYLVESTER***'s mouth.)*

SCAPINO. Honor, respect, deference to a father – these are all very important, and of course when I heard what your son had done my reaction was the same as yours. In fact, the first thing I did when I got wind of what your son was up to was to walk right up to him and give him a piece of my mind on *your* behalf.

DON ALBERT. I thank you.

SCAPINO. But then I took a step back and thought about it. And you know what? It's not as bad as you might initially think.

DON ALBERT. Are you an idiot? How is going against me and marrying some stranger without my consent not as bad as I might think?

SCAPINO. Well, when you think about it, Octavio's just following his *destiny*.

DON ALBERT. Following his... *(Laughs.)* Oh Scapino. Scapino, Scapino...I'm disappointed in you. That's the best you can do? He was *destined* to marry this girl? What kinda lawyer were you? Follow that logic to its conclusion and anyone can justify doing whatever they want: lie, cheat, steal, whatever. I'd love to see some stooge tell the judge, "I'm sorry, your honor, yes it's true. I iced all of 'em! But don't worry about it! I was just following my *destiny*." No wonder you ended up in the pokey.

SCAPINO. Don Albert, you hurt me. And what's worse, you misunderstand me. This is *me* telling *you* how *he* got mixed up in all of this is nothing short of *destiny*!

DON ALBERT. All right, I'll bite. How the hell did he get mixed up with this?

SCAPINO. Well here's the thing. He's young. *You* had to learn from the school of hard knocks, but he's a mere babe, a youth. He doesn't have half your street smarts. Kids, am I right? They leap before they look. Like, for instance, Don Jerry Geronte's son, Leo – I've tried to keep him outta trouble for as long as I can remember, and still, I come to find out he's ended up in much worse of a fix than your son –

DON ALBERT. *Worse* fix? What do you mean?

SCAPINO. But we grow up and we have to make mistakes or we'll never learn. Right? I mean, I bet even you were young once.

DON ALBERT. Well...

SCAPINO. I bet you were. I bet you have some stories from when you were a young stallion of a man. I bet you came, you saw, you conquered the fairer sex on a regular basis. You devil, you cad, you rapscallion, you. You dog. Woof. I bet you cut quite the figure when you were working the ladies back in Hoboken.

DON ALBERT. I might have, Scapino. I might have.

SCAPINO. You devil. You dog. Woof.

DON ALBERT. All right, yes. You got me. I did. I don't deny I was a stallion with the ladies.

SCAPINO. Woof. Neigh.

DON ALBERT. Heh heh. Wait a minute, don't distract me. I never did as stupid a thing as he did. Never in my life.

SCAPINO. But Don Albert, with respect, what could he have done? He meets this girl who can't resist his irresistible sexiness (he gets that from you by the way) and who he can't take his eyes off of (he gets that from you too, you know, you dog, you stallion, woof woof, neigh neigh). He courts her: he puffs and he flaunts, he struts and he warbles, he smooches and he canoodles. She is no match for his fragrant charms and she yields to his advances! And then, in the throes of passion, in barges her pop – none other than the chief of police of Boca!

DON ALBERT. No.

SCAPINO. Yes!

DON ALBERT. They're tough in Boca.

SCAPINO. There he was, staring down the loaded barrel of a service-issued law enforcement revolver. He had to think quick! He had to choose between an angry father back at home or an angry father right in front of him. Code Red! Code Red! What could he do? He told her father they were engaged, and that his intentions were nothing but mostly honorable. And you know what? Her father drove them to the courthouse that very day!

DON ALBERT. *(To* **SYLVESTER**.*)* He was forced to get married?

(He removes the gag from **SYLVESTER***'s mouth.)*

SYLVESTER. Yes he was. I swear it. I swear.

*(***DON ALBERT** *stuffs the gag back into* **SYLVESTER***'s mouth.)*

DON ALBERT. Octavio should have reached out to the family. We would have taken care of things for him.

SCAPINO. That's just what he didn't want to do.

DON ALBERT. Well, it would have made things easier for me to break the marriage up.

SCAPINO. Don Albert, with respect, you will do no such thing.

DON ALBERT. I won't?

SCAPINO. You will not.

DON ALBERT. So my son is forced to marry this girl by some jake in Boca and I am just to sit here and do nothing?

SCAPINO. Exactly. Besides, Octavio won't let you.

DON ALBERT. Oh, really. He won't let me.

SCAPINO. No, he won't. You want him to face the family as a coward? To admit he married this girl out of fear? What will your enemies say if your son shows such weakness? This might be the perfect opportunity for them to pounce. To test your strength! The shame.

DON ALBERT. So what?

SCAPINO. For the sake of the family, Don Albert, Octavio needs to be able to hold his head high and tell people he married this girl because he wanted to. Not because he had to.

DON ALBERT. And it's for the sake of the family that he needs to say the complete opposite. He's gonna marry Don Jerry's daughter.

SCAPINO. He won't do it.

DON ALBERT. He will, or it's his funeral.

SCAPINO. You wouldn't.

DON ALBERT. I would.

SCAPINO. You're a softy when it comes to your son.

DON ALBERT. I am not a softy.

SCAPINO. A marshmallow.

DON ALBERT. No.

SCAPINO. A teddy bear.

DON ALBERT. Stop it.

SCAPINO. Forgive me, Don Albert, but I know deep, deep, *way deep* down, you are a good man.

DON ALBERT. Let me explain something to you, Scapino, and I will use very small words so that you can understand. I am not a good man. I am a bad, *bad* man. I am a bastard man. Now you go fetch my embarrassment of a son from the rock he's hiding under and bring him home to me. I want to talk some sense into him before I have to get unpleasant.

SCAPINO. Right away.

DON ALBERT. Sylvester, you mollusk, go and help him.

SYLVESTER. Yes, Don Albert. Right away, Don Albert.

   (He exits in haste.)

DON ALBERT. Meanwhile, I'm gonna talk to Don Jerry and think of some way to fix this mess to my advantage. Scram.

(**SCAPINO** *exits in haste.*)

DON ALBERT. God in heaven! For the love of all that's holy, why did you leave me with this halfwit of a son? Is this punishment for my almost legal lifestyle? Why couldn't it have been Octavio swept out to sea all those years ago instead of my little girl? My tiny angel? My little pudding princess? I'm sure a daughter would have been much easier to raise than a son.

(*He exits.*)

Scene Five

(SCAPINO and SYLVESTER re-enter in excited haste. SCAPINO is rejuvenated. SYLVESTER is relieved.)

SYLVESTER. Holy mackerel, Scapino! I thought it was curtains for me. You got me off the hook!

SCAPINO. For now, Sylvester.

SYLVESTER. You just spinned him this way and that. Like one of those spinner things that spins round and round and round and round and round and round when you spin them.

SCAPINO. A top?

SYLVESTER. Yeah, that. You're an artist.

SCAPINO. And I'm just getting started.

SYLVESTER. Beautiful. So what do we do now?

SCAPINO. Just leave it to me, Sylvester. I got a plan. We need money. We're broke and I gotta pile up some cash if we're gonna skip outta town and set ourselves up someplace respectable. Somewhere away from these knuckleheads.

SYLVESTER. *(Wistfully.)* Grover's Corners.

[Note: The rest of this scene is the Chicago version. In the second production it was Pittsburgh. Feel free to change your production's shining city on the hill to taste, with accompanying appropriate geographical references.]

SCAPINO. I told you, Sylvester, that's not a real place. But we'll find someplace nice. Someplace where an honest fella can set himself up without worrying about getting whacked by his best pal, or sent up the river by his so-called family. Someplace honest. Someplace peaceful. Like Chicago.

SYLVESTER. City of Brotherly Love!

SCAPINO. That's Philadelphia.

SYLVESTER. Wild and Wonderful!

SCAPINO. That's West Virginia.

SYLVESTER. Go Bears?

SCAPINO. *(Begins scanning the audience.)* Exactly. But what I need right now is a partner in crime to trick Don Albert into giving us some cash. Someone devious and crafty who can transform into another person entirely. A chameleon. A mastermind.

SYLVESTER. Gee, I wonder who that could be.

SCAPINO. *(A good portion of this is impov and can be ad-libbed to taste.)* Excellent, Sylvester, glad you volunteered. You'll do nicely. And you're all I've got... Now, stand up straight. I'm gonna teach you how to act like a villain...a dangerous monster. Give me some attitude. Like so. Yeah. Now pull your hat down over one eye. Get shady. Nice. Get mean. Good. Now put some swagger in your walk. Not too much swagger – you look like Bob Fosse got struck by lightning. Better. Hands at your side. Mean! Face like a killer. Meaner. Crazy eyes. Crazier! Not bad. Not bad at all. Good, good, Sylvester. I think we need to dig a little deeper. I'm gonna tear you down so I can build you back up. I think we need to channel your angry spirit animal. Dig deep Sylvester. Gimme a –

> *(He suggests two animals ["Gimme an angry chipmunk," "Give me an incensed poodle," "Now gimme a furious dolphin," "An enraged manatee," etc.] that* **SYLVESTER** *acts out, and then* **SCAPINO** *asks the audience for suggestions.* **SYLVESTER** *acts out each animal as suggested, then* **SCAPINO** *asks him to channel them together and act out all the animals at once.)*

All right, excellent Sylvester, I think you're ready for your meeting with Don Albert. It'll be the performance of a lifetime!

SYLVESTER. Oh, no, Scapino. Please don't get me killed.

SCAPINO. Easy, Sylvester.

SYLVESTER. I mean, he gives my heebie-jeebies the heebie-jeebies.

SCAPINO. Just follow the plan and we're golden.

SYLVESTER. Oh, God...

SCAPINO. C'mon! Live a little, Sylvester! We're in this together. You and me. Chicago or bust. Just feel that swagger. You feelin' it?

SYLVESTER. I think I feel it... Oh, my... I feel it, Scapino!

SCAPINO. Nice, Sylvester! Chicago, here we come.

> (**SCAPINO** *and* **SYLVESTER**'s *swagger turns into a swaggery dance to the tune of something in the style of "Jeepers Creepers."* They dance together offstage.*)

---

*A license to produce *Scapino* does not include a performance license for "Jeepers Creepers." The publisher and author suggest that the licensee contact ASCAP or BMI to ascertain the music publisher and contact such music publisher to license or acquire permission for performance of the song. If a license or permission is unattainable for "Jeepers Creepers," the licensee may not use the song in *Scapino* but should create an original composition in a similar style or use a similar song in the public domain. For further information, please see Music Use Note on page 3.

ACT TWO

Scene One

(**DON ALBERT** *and* **DON JERRY GERONTE** *enter from opposite sides of the stage – their thin veneer of politeness masks a tense and dangerous intent. This veneer slowly disintegrates as the scene progresses. Each carries a briefcase.*)

DON GERONTE. Don Albert. It is a pleasure.

DON ALBERT. Don Jerry Geronte. The pleasure is mine.

DON GERONTE. I must confess, Don Albert, the news I am hearing about my future son-in-law is causing me no small amount of indigestion. My patience thins.

DON ALBERT. Don Jerry, I speak to you as a gentleman. What you hear is nothing. It is a trifle. A tiny obstacle that will be swept away by nightfall. You got nothing to worry about.

DON GERONTE. I am in some small way relieved to hear that, Don Albert. And please receive my response with all of the respect and admiration due a fellow Don... I will believe it when I see it.

DON ALBERT. You will see it soon enough, Don Jerry. Now please enlighten me as to the whereabouts of this daughter of yours whom my son is supposed to marry? My boys tell me they have not yet heard of her arrival to Naples. A more suspicious man might question whether this might be some kind of setup, or whether this so-called daughter-in-hiding exists at all.

DON GERONTE. Allow me to put your suspicions to rest, Don Albert. My boys are on their way to fetch her as we speak.

DON ALBERT. But where is she?

DON GERONTE. Tut tut, my friend. You know I have her and her mother hidden for their own protection. In our profession we can never be too careful. Put your mind at ease, Don Albert, our kids will be married this very night. That is, if your son is a man and not a no-good piece of filth that will get what's coming to him if he's done what I'm told he's done.

DON ALBERT. As I said to you, Don Jerry, you're misinformed. You have my word as a gentleman.

DON GERONTE. A *gentleman*. You know what I think, Don Albert?

DON ALBERT. No, Don Jerry. What do you think?

DON GERONTE. I think the fish rots from the head first. I think the lack of character exhibited by a no-good, two-timing son is the result of a shoddy upbringing.

DON ALBERT. I am having difficulty understanding your meaning, Don Jerry Geronte. Please enlighten me.

DON GERONTE. Gladly. I mean that if you had been a better father and brought up your son to show some deference to his betters and not flit around like some Casanova clown, he wouldn't have disrespected you in the way that he has. And we wouldn't be having this polite conversation.

DON ALBERT. I see. Thank you, Don Jerry, for explaining your meaning. And hypothetically speaking, what would you have done if you had caught *your* son in such a disrespectful situation as mine?

DON GERONTE. Besides copping up to my shame and getting down on my knees to beg forgiveness from those whom he has wronged by his actions? I would teach my son a lesson in respect that he would not soon forget.

DON ALBERT. I see. Thank you for your wisdom, my friend. And your son, Leo? How is that model example of forthright character doing?

DON GERONTE. Good. Why?

DON ALBERT. No reason, Don Jerry. It's just that one might question your well-intentioned yet hypocritical lesson in upbringing if, for instance, *your* son had been up to something while we were away that was even more shameful and disrespectful than mine.

DON GERONTE. What are you telling me, Don Albert?

DON ALBERT. Just that it's sometimes wise for someone to clean the smudged glass of one's own house and take a good, long look at what's going on in there before they begin throwing rocks at someone else's. Respectfully.

DON GERONTE. Are you saying my son has done something I should know about?

DON ALBERT. Maybe he has, maybe he hasn't. But why should you worry, Don Jerry Geronte, you brought him up to be just like you, so I'm sure he's every bit the man his father is.

DON GERONTE. All right, knock it off! What have you heard?

DON ALBERT. Your man Scapino has loose lips, but he didn't give me any details.

DON GERONTE. Scapino?

DON ALBERT. Scapino. So why don't you ask him? In the meantime, I'm gonna go and get my son ready for tonight's wedding. Good luck, Don Jerry Geronte. I hope your daughter gets here soon. Let's hope for both our sakes that nobody screws this deal up.

(He exits.)

Scene Two

DON GERONTE. Leo Geronte...what the hell did you do? Whoa...calm down, Jerry, take it easy. If Leo *didn't* do... whatever it is Scapino said he's done...okay! But if he did and screwed this deal up for me somehow? I'll kill him!

> (**LEO** *enters excitedly.*)

LEO. Pop! You're home!

DON GERONTE. *(Warmly.)* Leo! Son! Hugs!

> (*He waits for* **LEO** *to get within striking distance, then grabs him by the face.*)

I'll kill yah!

LEO. Ow! Pop! You're hurting my face.

DON GERONTE. This is just the beginning. Siddown. Look at me. In the eyeballs.

LEO. Yessir.

DON GERONTE. What's been goin' on with you?

LEO. With me?

DON GERONTE. *(Pulls a small bottle out of* **LEO**'*s pocket.*) With you. Ah ha! What is this?

> (**LEO** *takes cologne bottle or something like Axe body spray from* **DON GERONTE** *and sprays it generously on himself to demonstrate.* **DON GERONTE** *takes it back.*)

Shaddup.

> (*He proceeds to spray* **LEO** *in the eyes several times.*)

Don't be a wiseguy. If you did what I don't know you did yet, but if what I don't know you did is worse than what I hears your friend did? You're *done.*

LEO. Done?

DON GERONTE. Dead. Get it?

LEO. Got it. But I ain't done nothin' Pop.

DON GERONTE. *(Threatening.)* Nothin'?

LEO. Wait... Wait... Well, I... Nope.

> **(DON GERONTE** *makes things physically unpleasant for* **LEO.)**

DON GERONTE. You sure about that?

LEO. Ow! Pop! I've been good! I've been a good boy!

DON GERONTE. Scapino sings a different tune.

LEO. *(Scowling.)* Scapino...

DON GERONTE. Why do you say his name like that?

LEO. Like what?

DON GERONTE. *(Scowling.)* Scapino...

LEO. *(Scowling.)* Scapino... No reason.

DON GERONTE. I shoulda put him in the ground instead of serving him up to the feds on a silver platter. Listen up, Leo. Be home in an hour. If Scapino's right, and I find out you done what he says you done I don't yet know you did? You're dead.

LEO. Dead?

DON GERONTE. *Done.*

> *(He exits.)*

Scene Three

LEO. Scapino! That rat. What did he tell Pop? If Scapino told Pop I did what I don't know I did… Wait… If I didn't do what Scapino doesn't know I didn't done… Wait… If… Forget it. I'm gonna kill Scapino.

(**OCTAVIO** *and* **SCAPINO** *enter.*)

OCTAVIO. *(To* **SCAPINO.***)* Thank you my friend, thank you. This is genius. I owe you my life.

SCAPINO. It's nothin'.

LEO. You!

SCAPINO. Oh, hi Leo. What's up?

LEO. I'm gonna pop your head like a zit.

(*He grabs* **SCAPINO**'s *head to pop it like a zit.* **OCTAVIO** *tries unsuccessfully to intervene.*)

SCAPINO. Ow! Mercy!

OCTAVIO. Leo! What's going on?

LEO. I'll kill you, stoolie! Admit it!

SCAPINO. Ack! Admit what?

LEO. Don't play stupid, stupid!

OCTAVIO. Leo! Calm down!

LEO. Admit it or I'll…

(*He gets* **SCAPINO** *in a compromising position.*)

SCAPINO. Okay! Okay! I admit it! Remember a couple days ago when you came home and your liquor cabinet was smashed open and all those priceless bottles of thirty-year-old single malt scotch had shattered and spilled all over the shag carpet and I told you the cat did it?

LEO. Mr. Whiskers was a bad kitty.

(*They all make the sign of the cross.*)

SCAPINO. Well, it was me what drank that scotch and pinned it on Mr. Whiskers to cover my tracks. Forgive me!

LEO. You scumbag! But that's not what I'm talking about! Admit it!

SCAPINO. That's all I can remember!

LEO. I'll kill you!

> *(He beats* **SCAPINO** *again.)*

OCTAVIO. Leo!

SCAPINO. All right, you got me! I admit it! Remember yesterday when you gave me the keys to that shiny shimmery new Camaro you bought for that pretty young girl you're in love with and told me to drive it over to her and present it as a gift and I came back with a bloody lip and covered in dirt and told you that I was beaten and carjacked by the Scaramouch family? Well, nobody touched me. I just kept the Camaro.

LEO. You kept it?

SCAPINO. Yes.

LEO. Why?

SCAPINO. …To drive?

LEO. Bastard! I whacked three Scaramouches because of that! You lying, thieving, jerkface! I'll get you for that! But that's still not what I'm talking about, either. Admit it!

> *(He beats* **SCAPINO** *again, again.)*

SCAPINO. Oh…

LEO. Ah ha! Spill it! Have a clear conscience before you meet your maker!

SCAPINO. All right! All right! I admit it! Remember that masked burglar who broke into the house six months ago? And who woke you up by beating you with a big knobby stick and who chased you around the house with that stick and kept hitting you and hitting you as you tried to run away and then you fell down the stairs and thought you had broken your spine?

LEO. Of course I remember.

SCAPINO. That was me. I was that burglar.

LEO. You?

SCAPINO. I –

LEO. I'll kill you!

SCAPINO. I only wanted to scare you so that you would always remember to lock your doors at night! It was a teaching moment! It's not safe out there.

LEO. *(Pulling a knife and threatening* **SCAPINO.***)* I will not forget a single slight you have visited upon me, Scapino. I'm gonna peel your face off like an onion. Revenge will be slow and sweet. But before you die just tell me what I want to hear. Tell me what you said to my pop today?

SCAPINO. Your pop? Don Jerry Geronte? I haven't seen him since he got back.

LEO. Liar!

SCAPINO. I swear! He'll back me up! I swear!

LEO. No, he won't! He told me everything. You ain't got no loyalty to nothin' and nobody!

SCAPINO. Leo, I swear on my mother's rosary...he wasn't telling you the truth.

Scene Four

(A distraught **SYLVESTER** *enters.)*

SYLVESTER. *(To audience.)* Mayday! I'm dead. I'm doomed. I gotta hide! When Leo finds out, I'm a doomed dead man.

LEO. Finds out what?

SYLVESTER. *(Nonchalantly to* **LEO.***)* Oh hi, Leo.

(He realizes who he's talking to.)

Leo! Oh, my God! Please don't whack me! It's not my fault! Your lady friend? The girl you're in love with? The girl who means everything to you?

LEO. Yeah?

SYLVESTER. The gypsies! The gypsies have taken her! They've taken your lady friend, Leo.

OCTAVIO. Gypsies?

LEO. In Florida?

SYLVESTER. I swear! I'm telling you! They say if you don't give in to their demands by nightfall, they're sticking her in the back of their Volkswagen and heading home to Woodstock!

LEO. Woodstock?

SYLVESTER. Or was it Burning Man…

SCAPINO. *(Beat.)* HIPPIES. Hippies, Sylvester. Not gypsies.

SYLVESTER. That's what I said! They said their van is broke down and they didn't sell nearly as many hemp bracelets as they hoped they would down here. They're taking her back to Woodstock unless you pay up!

LEO. Oh no!

OCTAVIO. What's the big deal?

LEO. It's her family! They raised her as a little foundling girl in a commune in the Catskills! They're totally off the grid! I'll never find her if that van makes it out of town!

OCTAVIO. So just whack 'em.

LEO. Never! I'm their future son-in-law! I gotta be on the up-and-up about this or she'll never forgive me. Scapino! Scapino my friend, my pal, my savior! Help me! I beg you! Here, let me fix your collar…

SCAPINO. Friend? Nice! I'm your friend now? First you slap me around and now you slap me on the back, is that it?

LEO. I, I, I forgive you, Scapino. Everything. The scotch, the Camaro…

SCAPINO. The beating?

LEO. *(Angry.)* You son of a…
(Recovering…friendly-like.) What are you even talking about? What beating? See? I've forgotten everything. All in the past. What's done is done, pal. Friend. And anything you might do in the future. Even if it's worse. But help me!

SCAPINO. Nah, that's okay. Now, where were we? I should lie down so you can start kicking me again. It's more than I deserve and you're such a tough guy…

LEO. Forgive me Scapino! Please! If I murder you, you can't save me!

SCAPINO. Nah, I'm useless.

LEO. No, you're a gem! A genius! Save me!

OCTAVIO. C'mon Scapino, you have to.

SCAPINO. Did you not just see what he did to me? I think he broke a lung.

LEO. I was a bastard. A hothead. I deserve nothing. But look into your heart Scapino. Look right in there. Help me. I beg you.

SCAPINO. You were gonna *kill* me.

LEO. Yeah, I'm sorry. It's my go-to.

SCAPINO. I'm not even insured.

LEO. *(Dejected.)* You're right. I follow my heart, Scapino, and this is where it gets me. I'm a worthless fiery bull of destruction. Here. Here is my breast bared. Take a knife. I deserve it. Stick it in my heart. Strike, Scapino! End my despair!

OCTAVIO. Jesus, Mary, and Joseph, Scapino! Forgive him!

SCAPINO. Well…all right. Get up, I forgive, I forgive. Only next time don't be such a meathead.

LEO. Thank you, Scapino! Thank you! Now promise me you'll help me save my Feather.

SCAPINO. Excuse me, what?

LEO. Promise me.

SCAPINO. Help you save who?

LEO. Feather.

SCAPINO. Feather?

LEO. Feather.

OCTAVIO. Feather.

LEO. Feather.

SCAPINO. Feather?

SYLVESTER. It's a name.

LEO. Feather.

SCAPINO. *Feather.* Ah…and where did you meet Feather.

LEO. At Lollapalooza. We have so much in common.

(Beat.)

SCAPINO. I see. *(To* **SYLVESTER.***)* And how much does he need to get her back from the gypsies?

SYLVESTER. Hippies.

SCAPINO. Hippies?

SYLVESTER. Fifty grand.

SCAPINO. Fifty grand to fix a VW Van?

SYLVESTER. It's vintage.

SCAPINO. Got it. And, Octavio, how much do you need to make a getaway and honeymoon in style?

OCTAVIO. In style? Twenty green.

SCAPINO. Great. So I squeeze fifty out of Leo's pop and thirty out of your pop, that makes…

OCTAVIO. I said I only need twenty.

SCAPINO. What, you think I work pro bono?

OCTAVIO. Heh, bono. I like your style, Scapino.

LEO. I don't get it.

SCAPINO. *(Aside to audience.)* And he won't get any of it when I pull this little caper off.

LEO. *(Confused.)* What'd you say?

SCAPINO. Nothing, go back to sleep. Octavio, our plan is underway so let's proceed carefully. Don Albert is crafty but he's on the hook. Leo, your pop will be even easier. He's as cheap as they come but he's never let his brain get in the way of what he was thinking.

LEO. I still don't get it.

SCAPINO. Exactly. Like father like son. What a family. Who knew a garden gnome could mate with a gorilla?

LEO. *(Furious.)* I'll rip your little... *(Recovering...friendly-like.)* This guy! I like you, Scapino. I really do.

SCAPINO. Good boy. Now that that's cleared up. You two amscray. I think I see Don Albert heading this way and it's time to work a little magic.

> *(***OCTAVIO*** and ***LEO*** exit.)*

Sylvester.

SYLVESTER. Yeah, boss?

SCAPINO. Quick, go get into your disguise. I need you on standby in case things start to go south with Don Albert.

SYLVESTER. To do the thing we practiced?

SCAPINO. Yeah, you're my ace in the hole.

SYLVESTER. That's disgusting...

SCAPINO. Forget it – just watch for the signal. You thespian! You Olivier!

SYLVESTER. *(As he exits.)* Doomed...

SCAPINO. Just remember your spirit animal...

> *(***SYLVESTER*** *briefly channels his animal from earlier as he exits.)*

Excellent! Ah, here he is.

Scene Five

(**DON ALBERT** *enters.*)

DON ALBERT. Oh hello, Scapino. Where's my son?

SCAPINO. I'm still lookin'. *(Looks around casually.)* Nope. You're still mad at him, aren't you?

DON ALBERT. It's that obvious? I'm a wreck. The indignity and betrayal is eating me alive. Only my love of Octavio's poor, dear, recently dead mother, God rest her soul, is keeping me from breaking every bone in his body.

SCAPINO. Whoa whoa whoa. You know the drill, Don Albert. You whack your own son and there will be questions. Especially since his young bride's pop is a cop. There'll be an investigation! You don't want to get mired in the fetid swamp of our criminal justice system, do you?

DON ALBERT. Patooie.

SCAPINO. My sentiments exactly. But I must say the pain in your heart has touched me, Don Albert, it really has. And so on your behalf I have been noodling a way out of this that leaves both you and your son's honor intact, and I think I've found it...

DON ALBERT. You have? Tell me Scapino! I'm all ears.

SCAPINO. Well, I took the liberty of contacting this young girl's very angry policeman father...well, he was furious – he doesn't have one ounce of your patience, your dignity, your steely calm in the face of adversity.

DON ALBERT. Few do, Scapino.

SCAPINO. He told me he should have pumped your son full of lead the moment he saw him. Well, I calmed him down – I told him your predicament, and of your deep love as a father as well as your respect for the badge...

DON ALBERT. Patooie.

SCAPINO. Patooie, indeed. Owing to your stature as a wealthy, almost respectable pillar of the Naples community – he would be willing to forgive and forget...for a small pledge of generosity on your part.

DON ALBERT. How much.

SCAPINO. Well the first number he threw out there was crazy-talk.

DON ALBERT. How much.

SCAPINO. I mean, bonkers...looney-tunes.

DON ALBERT. Tell me how much or I'll break your legs.

SCAPINO. Thirty large. Cash.

DON ALBERT. THIRTY LARGE? *(He sputters.)*

SCAPINO. That's just what I said, but *he* said he needed the dough. He dumped all of his savings into a Frozen Yogurt business that went south and he needs to pay off a lot of debt – the yogurt alone set him back ten grand.

DON ALBERT. All right, ten I can do.

SCAPINO Then there's the sprinkles, the gummy bears, the nuts, the cherries-on-top.

DON ALBERT. All right fifteen grand and we're done.

SCAPINO. That's generous.

DON ALBERT. I think so.

SCAPINO. Then there's the Yogi-Mobile that brought a delicious low-fat frozen treat to the neighborhood children.

DON ALBERT. He can drive it into a brick wall for all I care. I ain't paying for no Yogi-Mobile.

SCAPINO. But the driver of that Yogi-Mobile was such a sad old soul, desperate for someone to give him a leg up during these brutal economic times and who brought yogurt-y joy to bright smiling faces –

DON ALBERT. All right thirty grand.

SCAPINO. – And who unfortunately wasn't legally allowed within fifty feet of a school or playground.

DON ALBERT. That's it! I'm gonna settle this my way! To hell with the cops or the courts!

SCAPINO. The courts! You don't want to tangle with the courts! It's a madhouse! A labyrinth of lies, deceits, and *lawyers.* It'll eat you up and spit you out like a cat with a hairball. You better brush up on your legal-speak if you hope to talk your way out of this mess, Don Albert. You've got your habeas corpus and onus probandi and ipso factos and ex post factos and all de factos and heaven help you if you're caught in flagrante delicto. I mean you'd have to be non compos mentis! Cui bono?

DON ALBERT. Cui bono?

SCAPINO. Gesundheit.

DON ALBERT. Whatever – so I'll pay 'em all off.

SCAPINO. You're gonna have to grease a lot of palms, Don Albert. Remember, her pop is a cop. They're *all* gonna be against you. You gotta pay the bailiff not to whisper into the judge's ear. You gotta pay your defense to keep them from commiserating with counsel and selling you to Sing Sing. You'll have to pay off the prosecutor to undermine the evidence. "If the glove don't fit"?! You gotta pay the paralegals and assistants and stenographers and interns by the hour while they seal and notarize, document and mimeograph every bit of baloney that's been argued and counter-argued, sustained and objectioned!

DON ALBERT. Objectioned?

SCAPINO. Overruled! And don't get me started on the judge! You're gonna have to stuff a lotta dough under his robes if you want him to bang a generous gavel. But what if he don't take, Don? What if he's squeaky clean? What if he's *untouchable*? Then you're guilty!

DON ALBERT. Guilty?

SCAPINO. It's the chair, Don Albert, THE CHAIR!

DON ALBERT. The chair? Pardon me, Scapino, but –

SCAPINO. Oh, there will be no pardons for you Don Albert! You better appeal! There's the district appeal and then the federal appeal and the appellate appeal and the appealing appeal and the court of appeals – appalling. And when you finally end up in front of the Supreme Court?! How many rounds of golf are you gonna have to throw pro bono for the Chief Justice of the United States of America to render a verdict in your favor?

DON ALBERT. ...How much was that yogurt again?

SCAPINO. For the yogurt and the sprinkles and the gummies, nuts, and cherries, plus the truck and the payouts to some very angry parents. It ends up being...hmmm... let's make it fifty and we'll call it even.

DON ALBERT. (*As he advances on* **SCAPINO**.) That copper's not getting a dime. When my boys get back into town this guy is gonna...

SCAPINO. (*Giving "the signal" to* **SYLVESTER**.) Too bad they're not, Don Albert, 'cause here "this guy" comes and he looks dangerous!

DON ALBERT. (*Quietly to* **SCAPINO**.) He does look dangerous. Quick, Scapino, give me your gun.

SCAPINO. I don't have a gun, Don Albert. Use your own.

DON ALBERT. Mine's getting detailed!

Scene Six

*(Enter **SYLVESTER** disguised as a police officer from Boca.)*

SYLVESTER. FREEZE SCUMBAGS! SPREAD 'EM, SCAPINO. You have the right to remain silent! Anything you say can and will be used against you in a court of LAW.

SCAPINO. I know the drill.

SYLVESTER. GOOD. You WILL tell me the residence of Mr. Don Albert, the no-torious crime boss and alleged father of one Octavio – defiler of my ONE AND ONLY DAUGHTER.

SCAPINO. Why do you wanna know?

SYLVESTER. YOU WILL CALL ME SIR!

SCAPINO. Yes sir!

SYLVESTER. OOH YEAH. THAT IS BETTER. Word on the street is he will not honor his obligations.

SCAPINO. Oh, I don't know about that, sir. He just doesn't want any part of your yogurt shenanigans.

SYLVESTER. GRRRR! DROP AND GIVE ME TWENTY, SCAPINO! This is not about the YOGURT! This is about HONORING THE BADGE! *AND* THE YOGURT.

SCAPINO. I understand, sir!

SYLVESTER. These fists are going to PUT OUT AN APB all over his FACE. And they will neither CEASE, nor DESIST!

SCAPINO. I don't know, sir. Don Albert has nerves of steel. He's not afraid of the likes of you.

SYLVESTER. GRRR. ARGH. WHAT? CLEAN MY BOOTS, INCHWORM! I will PERPETRATE a HEINOUS ACT OF HABEAS CORPUS ALL OVER HIS ENTIRE BODY! GRRRR. Where is he? Is that him behind you?

SCAPINO. Not at all, sir!

SYLVESTER. USE YOUR OUTSIDE VOICE! ARE YOU POSITIVE?

SCAPINO. Sir, yes sir!

SYLVESTER. He looks a lot like that daughter-defiler, OCTAVIO! Just MUCH, MUCH OLDER!

SCAPINO. Coincidence, sir! They go to the same gym!

SYLVESTER. SPEAK WHEN YOU ARE SPAKEN TO! Maybe they are accomplices in cahoots?

SCAPINO. Not at all, sir! They hate each other!

SYLVESTER. Enemies?

SCAPINO. Mortal enemies!

SYLVESTER. *(To* **DON ALBERT.***)* PUT YOUR HANDS WHERE I CAN SEE THEM, PERP!

(**DON ALBERT** *does.* **SYLVESTER** *shakes one.*)

YOU SIR, I HAVE PROBABLE CAUSE TO FEEL GOOD ABOUT. You hate that BASTARD, Don Albert?

(**DON ALBERT** *nods, terrified.*)

I CANNOT HEAR YOU, CHIPMUNK!

SCAPINO. Yes! He's saying yes!

SYLVESTER. Good! I swear on my life. On my HONOR. And on the SANCTITY OF THE BADGE. I will bring ACTUAL AND GRIEVOUS BODILY HARM down upon this shiftless MOPE, DON ALBERT.

SCAPINO. But he says when his boys get back into town he's gonna teach you a lesson you'll never forget...

DON ALBERT. *(Terrified.)* Zip it, Scapino!

SYLVESTER. I don't think you boys understand. What we have here is a failure to communicate!

(*He brandishes a howdy doody cap gun, and fires several "warning shots" into the air. Much of the rest of this can/should be directed to the audience.*)

BRING IT ON, SUNSHINE! I hope he comes at me with two dozen of his best DRUNK AND DISORDERLIES. I WILL STAND MY GROUND... AND THE GROUND I STAND UPON WILL BE HIS SENSELESS CORPSE! I HAVE TRAINED NIGHT AND DAY FOR THIS

MOMENT! MIRANDA RIGHTS? MIRANDA WRONGS! THERE WILL BE A RECKONING!

(He pulls out his billy club.)

You see this stick?! It whispers to me every night. It says, "Please papa-daddy. Please BATHE ME IN THE BLOOD OF YOUR ENEMIES!" I will TASE ALL OF YOU! You want a piece of me? Take that! More? YEAH! THIS IS *MY* FUNHOUSE, CLOWNS! It's a full-on ASSAULT and I am the DEADLY WEAPON! Feel my STICK, Don Albert! My FIST, ninja-woman! My STEELY BOOT, terrified crying child! TASE THEM TO THE LEFT! TASE THEM TO THE RIGHT! THERE WILL BE A FULL CAVITY SEARCH! ON ALL OF YOU!! EVERY SINGLE CAVITY WILL BE SEARCHED!! YES!!!!

SCAPINO. Whoa whoa! We surrender, we surrender! Snap out of it!

SYLVESTER. What? Oh. Oooh...yeah. Yes. Mmm. Got it? Grrr. Have a good day.

(He exits.)

SCAPINO. How many cavity searches, Don Albert? How many? And for what? Your pride? Wow. Good luck to you, sir.

DON ALBERT. Scapino?

SCAPINO. Yes?

DON ALBERT. I've been thinking.

SCAPINO. Yes?

DON ALBERT. Let's give him the yogurt money.

SCAPINO. Good idea.

*(**DON ALBERT** procures a briefcase full of money, either from some cleverly hidden spot onstage or from under an audience member's chair, etc. Whatever is the most fun.)*

DON ALBERT. I've got it here. Let's go find him.

SCAPINO. And you'll just tell him you weren't who you said you were? It might confuse and anger him. You should give it to me to give to him. Besides, once he's face-to-face with you he might ask for more.

DON ALBERT. It's a lot of dough, Scapino, and I hate all this sneaking around. I'd feel better to see the money go right into his hands.

SCAPINO. *(Deadly serious.)* Yeah, I get it. Here's the skinny, Don Albert. Either you trust me or you don't. If you think I'm playing you, and that I'm not on your side, then just tell me. I'll walk away. Finito. Done. Find some other patsy to risk life and limb to keep your family together and safe...

DON ALBERT. Wait, Scapino! Here.

SCAPINO. No. Go find Sylvester. You trust him. Have him deliver the cash.

DON ALBERT. Aw, come on. For God's sake. Here, take it. Don't make me beg.

(He gives **SCAPINO** *the cash.)*

Watch out, though. That guy's dangerous.

SCAPINO. Got it.

*(**DON ALBERT** exits.)*

Scene Seven

SCAPINO. One Don down. One to go. Speak of the devil…

> *(He wets his hair and dons a life jacket or costume piece of some sort to signify he's just washed ashore.* **DON GERONTE** *enters.)*

(As **DON GERONTE** *enters.)* Oh no! Terrible news! Oh, the humanity! Why, God?! How could you do that to a father? Poor Don Jerry! Woe is me!

DON GERONTE. What's he saying about me? Scapino…

SCAPINO. Where is Don Jerry Geronte?

DON GERONTE. Right here, what is it?

SCAPINO. Where is he that I might break his heart!

DON GERONTE. Hey, jackass, snap out of it. How ya been? What's the matter?

SCAPINO. I don't know how to tell you…

DON GERONTE. With your mouth.

SCAPINO. It's your son. Leo.

DON GERONTE. What about him?

SCAPINO. Something awful has happened to him. My heart breaks…

DON GERONTE. Awful? You better start talkin' or I'll…

SCAPINO. Okay! Okay! Why God? So you know the last time I saw Leo he was down in the dumps. A real wreck. I dunno why that could be – probably something you said to him that he couldn't get over but that's neither here nor there. I try not to pry. So I says to him, I says, "You need some fresh air and sunshine. Let's go down to the docks and beat up some sailors. That always cheers you up." So we stroll down to the Naples pier. What do we see out in the water, Don Jerry? You know what we saw?

DON GERONTE. No I don't. I'm askin'.

SCAPINO. A beautiful yacht bobbing in the waves, flying a Turkish flag! A Turkish yacht, Don Jerry! And dangling off the sides, waving and calling and winking, were the most beautiful sun-bathed beauties you ever did see. It was a sight, I tell you.

DON GERONTE. Va-va-voom.

SCAPINO. Right you are. So we're standing on the beach ogling the scenery when this bronzed goddess, this Helen of the Deep steps up out from beneath the lapping waves of the azure Gulf in a thong bikini and a wicked smile. She walks right up to us. What a nice gal she is, all small talk and jokes and compliments. She says that she's the daughter of a Turkish trillionaire! And that yacht out yonder? That yacht is hers! And they're all so lonely for company out there after traveling such a long, long way that wouldn't we like to join her? It's just a short row by dingy to the party of a lifetime.

DON GERONTE. Sounds great so far. Then what?

SCAPINO. Well of course we say sure! She says her dingy is ready to go in the water and that all we need to do is get in and give it a little push. She didn't need to ask twice. But as soon as Leo was in her dingy, she clubs me in the back of the head with an oar and tosses me overboard!

DON GERONTE. Never trust a lady in a dingy!

SCAPINO. I wake up with a lump on my head, the yacht gone, and a hastily scribbled note on the inside of my palm! It says if you don't pay the Turk 100,000 big ones, your son is gonna decorate the foyer of her palatial mansion in Istanbul like a bear rug with a bad haircut.

DON GERONTE. I don't believe you.

> (**SCAPINO** *quickly scribbles, then shows* **DON GERONTE** *a hastily scribbled note on his palm.*)

I believe you. Never trust a lady in a dingy!

SCAPINO. Your son had no idea, Don Jerry.

DON GERONTE. You find another dingy and you row out to that yacht and tell that Turk every cop in this town owes me a favor.

SCAPINO. The cops? I'm sure the yacht's in international waters by now.

DON GERONTE. Never trust a lady in a dingy.

SCAPINO. Sometimes a surprise dingy can lead to an adventure. But that's beside the point.

DON GERONTE. Lemme tell you the point, Scapino. The point is this. You take one for the family. You do your duty and you go find that Turkish Salami –

SCAPINO. – Salome –

DON GERONTE. That's what I said. And you tell her to send Leo back to me and you'll take his place until I've had time to raise enough cash to free you.

SCAPINO. Pardon me Don Jerry but how stupid do you think she is? You think she's gonna swap the son of the richest and most notorious Don in Naples for a pathetic jerk like me?

DON GERONTE. You're right. Never trust a lady –

SCAPINO. – In a dingy. Focus, Don Jerry! You gotta think! You got till nightfall to raise the dough.

DON GERONTE. How much was it again?

SCAPINO. One hundred Large.

DON GERONTE. One hundred LARGE? Does she have any idea how much that costs?

SCAPINO. I think she does or she wouldn't have asked for it.

DON GERONTE. Like I can just snap my fingers and come up with one hundred Gs.

SCAPINO. That unreasonable vixen.

DON GERONTE. Scapino, I gotta tell you something.

SCAPINO. What is it?

DON GERONTE. *You* know.

SCAPINO. …You might as well just say it, Don –

DON GERONTE. *(Grabs* **SCAPINO**'s *face.)* Never trust a lady in a dingy!

SCAPINO. You're right, Don Jerry. But how could your son know? If you're gonna save him, you haven't got much time.

DON GERONTE. All right here.

(*He gives* **SCAPINO** *a key.*)

SCAPINO. What's this.

DON GERONTE. It's a key to my villa.

SCAPINO. Okay.

DON GERONTE. I want you to go to my place.

SCAPINO. All right.

DON GERONTE. Walk through my villa to the lanai and past the pool. You gotta slip past my guard poodles unnoticed.

SCAPINO. Got it.

DON GERONTE. Go into my pool house. Make sure no one is following you.

SCAPINO. Of course.

DON GERONTE. Inside is a laundry basket full of fluffy towels and silk speedos.

SCAPINO. Great. So I look under the speedos and…

DON GERONTE. No. You take those speedos and you sell them on Craigslist. And you use that money to pay that bastard Turk.

SCAPINO. Are you nutty? What's the matter with you?

DON GERONTE. Those are my finest speedos.

SCAPINO. You won't get a buck-fifty for some used banana hammocks. Get a grip, Don Jerry, it's your money or his life!

DON GERONTE. Never trust a lady in a dingy.

SCAPINO. Drop the dingy, Jerry. Oh my poor friend Leo! To think what could be happening to you right now! But I can't make a father love, Leo! I've done all I can do.

DON GERONTE. Wait wait wait. All right, Scapino, I'll get the money.

SCAPINO. Then for God's sake, Don Jerry, go get it!

DON GERONTE. I will. A thousand clams.

SCAPINO. One Hundred. Thousand. Dollars.

DON GERONTE. That's what you get for dipping her dingy in the water.

SCAPINO. I agree, Don Jerry.

DON GERONTE. Why couldn't you two have just gone out for frozen yogurt!

SCAPINO. Bankrupt, Don Jerry.

DON GERONTE. Damn that dingy.

SCAPINO. Damn it indeed.

DON GERONTE. Oh, yeah, I just remembered. I just happen to have a suitcase full of cash that I hid around here in case of an emergency. Yep. Here it is.

> *(He pulls out a briefcase full of cash from a hiding place onstage or that he's been holding the whole time. During the following,* **SCAPINO** *holds the briefcase while* **DON GERONTE** *empties the cash from the case and stuffs it in his pockets, down his pants, etc.)*

Take it. One hundred grand. Now go save my son.

SCAPINO. I will sir.

DON GERONTE. And tell that Turkish succubus she's a bastard.

SCAPINO. Done, sir.

DON GERONTE. And a crook.

SCAPINO. I will.

DON GERONTE. And a scoundrel.

SCAPINO. Okay.

DON GERONTE. And I will be revenged!

SCAPINO. Done.

DON GERONTE. And get her number, she sounds like a good time.

SCAPINO. Yes, sir.

DON GERONTE. Well, go on then.

SCAPINO. Don Jerry...

DON GERONTE. Oh, for God's sake, Scapino, what the hell is it now?

SCAPINO. The money.

DON GERONTE. Yeah?

SCAPINO. The ransom.

DON GERONTE. Give it to her!

SCAPINO. You gotta give it to *me*.

DON GERONTE. What?

> *(He notices he's holding the cash and the briefcase is empty.)*

Oh. Of course, Scapino.

> *(He reluctantly puts the cash back in the briefcase.)*

You see how this whole situation has me turned around.

SCAPINO. Of course.

DON GERONTE. Never trust a...you know the rest. One hundred grand. It's killing me. Bastard Turks!

> *(He takes out his frustrations by beating* **SCAPINO** *with the briefcase full of money.)*

I will be revenged, Scapino. Read my lips.

> *(He mouths or spells the word D-I-N-G-H-Y.)*

> *(He throws the briefcase down at* **SCAPINO**'s *feet and exits.)*

Scene Eight

SCAPINO. *(As he takes a few stacks of bills from the briefcase and stuffs them in his pocket.)* Yeah, go on, you cheapskate numbskull brute. That's what you get for getting your kid to slap me around. For what? Sport? This will egg my nest quite nicely!

*(**OCTAVIO**, **CHLOE**, and **LEO** enter.)*

OCTAVIO. Did you get it?

LEO. Will Pop pay up?

SCAPINO. *(Opening Don Albert's briefcase for **OCTAVIO** to see.)* Here, Octavio, this is for you.

> *(He reaches into the briefcase and tosses a bundle of loose bills into the air. While **OCTAVIO** and **CHLOE** scramble to collect the money as it rains down, **SCAPINO** pockets the remaining cash still left in the briefcase.)*

OCTAVIO. Woah, Scapino! You're the best.

CHLOE. Yay! Money! *(Starts crying.)*

OCTAVIO. *(Turned on.)* Oh, Chloe…

> *(He and **CHLOE** make out.)*

SCAPINO. All right, all right you two. Take a shower.

> *(He hands **OCTAVIO** Don Albert's briefcase, then turns to **LEO**.)*

For you, Leo?

LEO. Yeah, Scapino?

SCAPINO. For you?

LEO. Yeah, Scapino? Yeah, yeah?

SCAPINO. For *you*, Leo?! I got nothin'.

LEO. What? I knew he'd never knuckle. Now I'll never get Feather back.

> *(He starts beating himself up.)*

Idiot. I'm an idiot!

SCAPINO. *(His conscience gets the better of him.)* I'm such a sucker. *(To* **LEO.***)* Wait, Leo. I just needed to know how much you loved this Feather. It was a test.

(He holds Don Geronte's briefcase out to **LEO.***)*

Here you go.

LEO. *(Taking the briefcase.)* Scapino, I don't believe it!

SCAPINO. Yeah, you're welcome.

LEO. Now I can save Feather! I take back every time I've tried to kill you, Scapino. I breathe again!

SCAPINO. Yeah, well, it was my pleasure to squeeze Don Geronte outta all that dough. Now we're fair and square.

LEO. Fair and square, Scapino! It's like poetic or something! Pop sells you out, I beat you up, you take Pop's money, I save Feather. Even Stevens.

SCAPINO. Excuse me, what?

LEO. Even Stevens. It's like poetic or something!

SCAPINO. No no no...that first part.

LEO. Oh, yeah, Pop sells you out. To the feds. That's why you lost everything including your future. But you knew, right?

OCTAVIO. Of course he knew. Everybody knew.

CHLOE. We knew in Boca.

LEO. Yeah, what am I thinkin'? Everybody knew. Yeah, business is business. Glad to know we're all fair and square, Scapino. *(To* **OCTAVIO** *and* **CHLOE.***)* This guy! Yo, Octavio, let's find that Volkswagen.

SCAPINO. Whoa whoa whoa, Leo, you still gotta tell your pop that you're gonna marry this girl. Lemme soften him up for you.

LEO. You'll soften him up?

SCAPINO. Oh, I'll soften him up all right. My way.

LEO. Whatever way you think best, pal. You're aces, Scapino.

OCTAVIO. C'mon, Chloe.

CHLOE. Bye, Scapino.

(They exit gleefully, leaving **SCAPINO** *alone.)*

SCAPINO. ...Don Jerry Geronte... Screw me once? Shame on you. Screw me twice? ...I'll kill you.

(Blackout.)

Intermission

ACT THREE

Scene One

(**SCAPINO** *enters at the end of intermission and begins setting up a trap for Don Geronte, then gestures for* **SYLVESTER**, **CHLOE**, *and* **FEATHER** *to enter as the houselights go out.* **SCAPINO** *exits off in the direction of the safe house as* **SYLVESTER** *and* **CHLOE** *enter, followed by* **FEATHER**.)

SYLVESTER. The safe house is just around the corner. Come on, Chloe. Feather, please keep up.

FEATHER. All right, yeah, don't rush me. I want to enjoy this last bit of sunlight before you cage me up like a prisoner.

SYLVESTER. It's only for a few days. Leo and Octavio thought you two should hide here together until Scapino untangles this mess.

CHLOE. And it'll give us some time to bond, Feather. I want to hear all about your harrowing tale of ransom and rescue from those frightening gypsies!

SYLVESTER. Hippies.

CHLOE. Hippies.

FEATHER. You know the word "gypsy" is offensive, right? Use Romani.

CHLOE. Romani? Oh, honey, we don't do sauce from a jar.
(*To* **SYLVESTER**.) She's got so much to learn.
(*To* **FEATHER**.) So tell me about your ransom and rescue! Tell me. Tell me, Feather. Tell me...

FEATHER. Okay, okay! You people are all so dramatic. Right. Well, they got the money, they fixed the van, they went back to Woodstock. End of story. Here, have a bracelet.

(She tosses a hemp bracelet to **CHLOE.***)*

CHLOE. Thank you. *(Starts to cry.)*

FEATHER. I'll hang here for now. But I need my space…the sun and the sky and the wind blowing through my hair. I don't know how long I can stay cooped up in a shack before I get antsy.

SYLVESTER. *(Hurt.)* It's not a shack. It's my home.

FEATHER. Whatever. Do you have Netflix?

CHLOE. Let this hemp bracelet be a ropy symbol of our blossoming friendship, Feather. I welcome you with open arms, sister from another mister. If the bond between us does not grow and flourish and we end up bitter enemies, it won't be because of me. It will be all your fault, I promise you.

FEATHER. Thanks, I think. Good on you, Chloe. I don't back away from a friendship, when it's sincerely offered.

CHLOE. What about love, Feather? Do you back away from love?

FEATHER. That's another story, Chloe. Love is dangerous. Love can destroy.

SYLVESTER. You got that right, Feather. You know what else can destroy? Don Geronte if he finds us standing out here in the open. We gotta go!

FEATHER. What's his sign? Is he a Sagittarius?

SYLVESTER. His only sign will be the sign of the cross he makes as he buries us. C'mon, we gotta go!

(He takes **FEATHER** *by the arm – she takes him down.)*

Mommy.

FEATHER. No manhandling, Sylvester. Peace and love man but this body is a temple and since when did you get permission to rub the Buddha?

CHLOE. Feather! Wow.

FEATHER. Ugh. I'm going back to the van.

>(**SCAPINO** *enters in haste, catching sight of* **FEATHER** *beginning to leave.*)

SCAPINO. Woah woah woah, Feather, Feather, Feather, let's talk! Sylvester, calm down a minute.

FEATHER. Yeah, sorry Sylvester. This whole scene has me on edge.

SYLVESTER. *(Outraged.)* Well, I never...

FEATHER. Here, have a bracelet.

SYLVESTER. *(Touched.)* Aw, thank you!

FEATHER. You got two minutes, Scapino, then I'm a leaf in the wind man.

SCAPINO. What's going on? Talk to me. I mean we've only just met but you've been a terror since Leo ransomed you from out of the back of that Volkswagen.

FEATHER. You're right, I have. Maybe it's that dangerous glint in his eye when he smiles at me, but I don't fully trust Leo, whatever his bullish charms.

SCAPINO. C'mon...he's a drooling puppy dog when he sees you. It's like having your own murderous pit bull scampering around at your heels wherever you go.

FEATHER. Aw...puppies. I don't know Scapino, when I'm with Leo it's like...chemistry...but then it's like... insanity! What am I doing here? You know, maybe I just don't want to be tied down. I'm a free spirit. I just want to laugh and be free. And I want to enjoy the moment. I just want to laugh and be free and enjoy the moment and engage in acts of nonviolent protest against a cruel and oppressive patriarchy that gerrymanders congressional districts to the detriment of a free and open democracy and forces us to eat genetically modified produce.

SCAPINO. That's a mouthful...

FEATHER. I want to explore the boundaries of the healing power of medical marijuana and go on a spirit journey with my pet python, Max.

SYLVESTER. You brought a python?

CHLOE. Oooooh…

FEATHER. I will not be bullied by my family to sell hemp no matter how environmentally conscious it is and Leo, however rugged and adorable he may be, *Leo* certainly can't buy my love with *money*. Money, hemp, they're just *things*, Scapino, ideas that lock us in cages and push us on the path to toiling for the materialistic, corporate hegemony. Love isn't a transaction, but love *is* earned, Scapino. Love takes courage. How can I trust that Leo loves me when he doesn't even have the courage to tell his own father?

SCAPINO. You're right, Feather. But his father is a dangerous man. Leo will find his courage, I promise. If I didn't believe he loved you, I'd have never agreed to help you both out. Stay. Please.

FEATHER. …Okay. If you say so. I'll stay, for now. But I need to see some action.

(*To* **CHLOE.**) Chloe, let's go. This standing around is killing me.

CHLOE. *Killing* you? Oh my God, Feather, it's like we're both feeling the same things. The fear, the pain, the joy, the delicious misery, we really *are* like sisters…

(*She starts to sniffle with joy and misery.*)

FEATHER. We're not the same, Chloe. At least you know who your parents are. The family who raised me has left town in a tricked-out van that my ransom paid for and my potential father-in-law is a materialistic sadist who needs some serious cleansing.

SCAPINO. And those are his good points. But you can't choose family any more than you can choose love.

CHLOE. Leo seems hopelessly devoted, at least.

FEATHER. Men are dogs – their eyes are only on you until they spot another squirrel waving her tail and looking to grab some nuts.

CHLOE. You're right. Love is such a bummer. If only we knew past any doubt who was "the one." If only we knew for certain who was our "happily ever after"...

SCAPINO. Begging your pardon, Chloe, but what could be more boring! I'll take a spicy meatball sandwich over a slice of white toast without butter any day. I want my love to be like trench warfare...let every bit of ground taken and given be fought for. That means we've earned every inch we've gained and bled for every inch we've lost. Together. What a dance. That's a life worth celebrating with someone.

FEATHER. Ugh. Who asked you for your opinion, Scapino? Ground beef and toast? Love as war? Any more mansplaining you'd like to do before you ride off into the sunset? There you go, Chloe, more words of advice from a generation that thought partially hydrogenated soybean oil and artificial sweeteners were a good idea. Your heart is in the right place, Scapino, but your time has passed. This is our generation. We'll find our own path to love.

(*To* **SCAPINO** *and* **SYLVESTER**.) Now take me to your prison-cage, Sylvester, and then go away.

(*To* **CHLOE**.) I'll have to sage.

SYLVESTER. Just don't take the plastic off the couches when we get there. And lock the door after me. And remember the secret knock I gave you so that you'll know it's us outside and not some crazed maniac killer?

CHLOE & FEATHER. Nope.

FEATHER. What is it again?

SYLVESTER. (*Exasperated.*) Ugh.

> (*He tries several knocks, or maybe he just tries to think of several knocks; either way it stresses him out.*)

It was... Or was it... No I got it, it's... Oh My God I've forgotten the secret knock! We're all gonna die!

FEATHER. Is he always this high-strung?

SCAPINO. Pretty much. All right. Have fun, you crazy kids. I got things to do. Sylvester, just come up with another knock.

SYLVESTER. So simple.

FEATHER. Wait. *(Sincerely.)* Thanks, Scapino. For what you're doing for Leo and me.

SCAPINO. Don't mention it. Go housetrain that pit bull.

FEATHER. And I do want to hear how you swindled Leo's father out of all that cash. Sounds like an amazing story. I promise to reward you with my complete attention and occasional ironic laughter.

SCAPINO. Sylvester can do the honors. I still have a bit of payback to visit upon Don Jerry Geronte. *(Points to his head.)* Something wicked this way comes, and I can't allow boasting of my past success to distract me from executing some sweet, sweet revenge.

SYLVESTER. You got Don Jerry's money, Scapino. Why can't you just let it go?

SCAPINO. Call it a heroic flaw. I've got a head for this, don't worry.

SYLVESTER. What use is a head when there's a bullet hole between the eyes. Think of the consequences.

SCAPINO. Consequences, schmonsequences. Stuff that talk right in the ear. Don Jerry crossed the Rubicon when he sent me up the river. Too far, Sylvester. I will be avenged.

SYLVESTER. Yeah. Put it on your tombstone.

FEATHER. We still need you, Scapino. Don't get killed.

SCAPINO. Don't worry. Get to the safe house. It'll all be over before you can explain to Chloe the difference between a vegan and a macrobiotic vegetarian.

CHLOE. I need to write that on my arm. Lemme get a Sharpie.

(SYLVESTER, CHLOE, *and* **FEATHER** *exit.)*

Scene Two

(**SCAPINO** *lays an open sack on the ground and hides a baseball bat somewhere onstage.*)

(*As he finishes,* **DON GERONTE** *enters.*)

DON GERONTE. Scapino. There you are. What's going on with my son? Has the dingy-woman brought him back?

SCAPINO. Don Jerry! Thank God I found you. Your son is safe and sound, but you, sir, *you* are in terrible danger! Where are your boys?

DON GERONTE. They're still out of town.

SCAPINO. Perfect.

DON GERONTE. Perfect?

SCAPINO. Perfectly awful! There's a turf war brewing in Naples, and everyone's gunning for you.

DON GERONTE. Oh no!

SCAPINO. The most notorious crime families in south Florida are rolling into Naples to take you down, Don! The town is swarming with cold-blooded killers!

DON GERONTE. Oh crap. What do I do?

SCAPINO. I'll save you, Don Jerry. We just need to get you to a safe house and...shhh. What was that? Oh no.

DON GERONTE. What? Don't leave me, Scapino!

(**SCAPINO** *runs off, leaving* **DON GERONTE** *alone and exposed for a moment.*)

(*Vulnerable.*) Scapino?

(**SCAPINO** *re-enters.*)

SCAPINO. It was nothing. I thought I saw one of them coming.

DON GERONTE. Oh no. This is it.

SCAPINO. They'll have to get through me first. I love you like a father and couldn't leave you to die like this.

DON GERONTE. I'm touched Scapino. I will reward you handsomely for this. This beautiful, tailor-made suit is yours, just as soon as I've gotten a little more mileage out of it.

SCAPINO. So generous. Wait, I've got it! The perfect way outta this! I just happen to have this sack here with me. Just get into it and make like a pile of stinky trash.

>*(**DON GERONTE** begins getting into the sack.)*

You cannot move! No matter what happens! Your life depends on this! Got me?

DON GERONTE. I got you, Scapino.

SCAPINO. Now I'm going to sling you over my shoulders and carry you to the safe house.

DON GERONTE. I like it. You're a genius, Scapino!

SCAPINO. Excellent, Don Jerry. *(Aside.)* You're gonna regret the way you've hurt me.

DON GERONTE. What was that?

SCAPINO. I said what a pretty egret, perched in that tree.

DON GERONTE. Because it sounded like you said...

SCAPINO. No time for witty banter, Don Jerry. Get in that sack, I said! Stay hidden! Make like a compost heap! And most importantly...

DON GERONTE. Don't move.

SCAPINO. Exactly. Oh no, here comes one of them! He looks dangerous! Keep still.

>*(He exits, then enters with a bat as he pretends*
>*to be other dangerous men as well as himself*
>*while **DON GERONTE** is in the sack.)*

"Top of the morning to you, everyone. Would any kind soul happen to know where that no-good snake in the grass Don Jerry Geronte is so that I can end his miserable life, would they?"

*(Aside to **DON GERONTE**.)* Oh no! It's Jimmy "Three-Fingers" McAllister!

DON GERONTE. Jimmy McWhoosis?

SCAPINO. Stay in that sack!

"You, sir. I'll give you a thousand kind words if you let me know where Don Jerry is." What possible reason would you have to want to find him, Mr. Jimmy

"Three-Fingers" McAllister, sir? "For the possible reason that his nose needs to pay up for the loan his mouth has been taking out all over town. I plan to bruise this here shillelagh with the tippety-top of his skull and drink a toast this evening to his dearly-departed memory." Don Jerry is a gentleman! He deserves respect and should not be beaten with a stick. "So you're a friend of his, eh?

(He hits the sack with a stick.)

Well then, take that! You lickarse! Lie down with dogs and you'll rise with fleas! Take it ya feckin' bastard ya!"

(He beats the sack with a bat as he pretends to get beaten.)

Oh! Ouch! No! Ow! Ack! Sir, please, stop! Ouch! Ack! Ow! "That was for Don Jerry. Pass it on, you enemy of Ireland. Goodbye."

*(**DON GERONTE** begins to stagger out of the sack.)*

DON GERONTE. Ouch Scapino, that really hurt. I can't take any more of this!

SCAPINO. I've been beaten all over! It's only a matter of time before I'm black and blue from head to toe.

DON GERONTE. What? He was hitting me! I could feel every swing of his shillelagh!

SCAPINO. He might have clipped you by accident but he was swinging at me.

DON GERONTE. That don't make sense.

SCAPINO. Here comes another one! You're on your own Don Jerry! I'm getting in the sack…

*(There is a lazzi where **SCAPINO** and **DON GERONTE** fight to be the one who gets into the sack.)*

DON GERONTE. No! My sack! Mine! MY SACK.

SCAPINO. You're a cruel man Don Jerry, but it's survival of the fittest, I guess. All right, I'll help you one more time. Oh no! Here he comes! He looks like a foreigner.

"Who is to you calling me foreigner?" Hello, sir. "I am proud American businessman and true patriot. I voted six hundred times in last election. Now please to tell me where is this Don Jerry Geronte?" No idea, my American friend. "Pleased I would be to have a conversation with him that will happily involve the beating with a big stick and then some mild poisoning as well as maybe dirty bomb placed in his pants. But will start with happy beating. Is my imagination or is sack moving?" What? "Is your hiding something from Vladimir of rural Pennsylvania God Bless America? Please to show me what is in sack." No offense, sir, but what's in my sack is none of your business. "You think Vladimir is soft American who fears to beating you? Let me teach you how we deal with the peoples like you in Mother Rural Pennsylvania!"

(He beats the sack brutally.)

Ouch! Ow! Ack! Ow! Please stop! Eek! "Vladimir hopes you have learned lesson you will not be soon forgetting." *(One final kick.)* "Proschay." Ugh. Rural Pennsylvanians.

DON GERONTE. *(Looking out of sack.)* He kicked me! I think I need to go to the hospital.

SCAPINO. *(Pushes **DON GERONTE** back into sack.)* Feeling bad, Don Jerry? That's a terrible predicament. Just awful. Because here come the Cubans! The Cubans are coming, Don Jerry!

DON GERONTE. When will it end?

SCAPINO. *(With all the subtlety of Al Pacino in* Scarface.*)* It'll never end, Don Jerry. Get back in that sack! "YOU WANT TO MESS WITH ME?" You can't make me talk! "OKAY. YOU WANT TO PLAY ROUGH? THEN SAY HELLO TO MY LITTLE FRIEND!"

> *(He bangs something metallic over **DON GERONTE**'s head or puts an empty oil drum over the sack and smacks it rapidly to simulate a machine gun attack.)*

Ow! Eek! Ouch! Yikes! The pain! "RUN, BAD HOMBRES! HERE COME THE MEANEST WOMEN SOUTH OF THE MASON-DIXON!

> *(Improv where **SCAPINO** jumps off the stage and selects three audiences members to be the three women. **SCAPINO** hands them each a pool noodle or rolled up newspaper or Playbill and gets them to beat **DON GERONTE**.)*

KATRINA, WILMA, AND IRMA!" Oh, no! "Where is Don Jerry Geronte?" I don't know! "I'm gonna make landfall over his entire body. Watch me surge, bitches!"

> *(**SCAPINO** or the audience members beat the sack mercilessly – he thanks them and says he underestimated their brutality as he ushers them back to their seats.)*

"Uh-oh, ladies, the Scaramouches are back in town. Clear out!"

(As the Scaramouches.) I see a little silhouetto of a Don...

> *(The **ENSEMBLE** pops out from various points on the stage.)*

ALL (EXCEPT SCAPINO). *(In operatic fashion.) SCARAMOUCHE! SCARAMOUCHE! THIS IS GONNA END BADLY!*

> *(**SCAPINO** dances with wild abandon as he beats the sack in a performance art-like danse macabre – as he is about to land the finishing blow, **DON GERONTE** pops out of the sack. Record scratch.)*

DON GERONTE. You...

SCAPINO. Oh. Awkward.

> *(He runs away.)*

DON GERONTE. You punk. You betrayer. I will destroy you for this. SCAPINO SLEEPS WITH THE FISHES!

Scene Three

(**DON GERONTE** *collapses in agony as* **FEATHER** *comes running in, catching her breath.*)

FEATHER. Oh thank God, I finally lost him. I couldn't take it anymore.

(*She starts laughing to herself.*)

DON GERONTE. (*In pain.*) Ohhh...

FEATHER. Woah, dude, are you okay? You look terrible.

DON GERONTE. He's killed me! I've been attacked!

FEATHER. Okay. Calm down, you're going to be okay. I'm a healer.

DON GERONTE. You're a doctor?

FEATHER. No, doctors are quacks and drug dealers. I'm a *healer*. I'm going to work on your aura.

DON GERONTE. My aura? Wait...

FEATHER. I'll just put your bag-house over here for safekeeping.

DON GERONTE. It's not my bag-house –

FEATHER. I think I have a crystal here...

(*She pulls out a big healing crystal.*)

DON GERONTE. Crystal? What –

FEATHER. Just pull that bad energy right out of you –

DON GERONTE. No, no. I need an ambulance...

FEATHER. You are *really* carrying some serious darkness, man...

DON GERONTE. What? Get away –

FEATHER. Sit down, I need to cleanse you –

DON GERONTE. Watch it. I'm a dangerous –

FEATHER. (*Dangerous.*) I SAID SIT THE HELL DOWN SO I CAN CLEANSE YOUR FRICKIN' AURA, BUDDY.

DON GERONTE. How much will it cost me?

FEATHER. It's my service to the universe. It's a calling. No charge.

DON GERONTE. It's a deal.

> (**FEATHER** *begins to heal* **DON GERONTE,** *whatever that is. Awkward silence.)*

FEATHER. Feel anything yet?

DON GERONTE. Pain.

FEATHER. You need to let your pain go. Think calm thoughts. Channel warm breezes and butterflies. Who beat you up? Were you panhandling?

DON GERONTE. I don't wanna talk about it.

FEATHER. Then just breathe.

DON GERONTE. I *am* breathing. *(Awkward beat.)* What were *you* running from?

FEATHER. Hah. Oh, man. The short run or the long run? The long run I'm running from is... I dunno, love, I guess? There's a guy who's sweet on me. So cliché. He's such a tough guy, kind of a meathead. A little like you, no offense. Only dateable and much, much younger. Not my type at all. But ever since Lollapalooza –

DON GERONTE. Lallalalala...lawhat?

FEATHER. I know, right? Lollapalooza. It's a concert. It's like a, it's an old person Coachella – ugh, what was I even doing there? They're all the same. Corporate America capitalizing on what they think are the ideals of suburban kids in Connecticut. Like all these heteronormative old white dudes sitting in a boardroom, think-tanking what youth culture means. Anyway, my family piled us in the van and made me go. But then I met him. And...he's just been so sweet, and kind...and he listens. But he's from here and I was raised outside of Woodstock and don't even know where I belong... Oh man! What am I even doing *here*? And where is that Camaro he said he'd get? He told me he was gonna buy me a *Camaro*. Wait. Why do I want a Camaro? Anyway, I've tried to push him away but he still protests he loves me. This guy loves me so much he got his con-artist buddy to swindle his dumb cheapskate of a father out of a hundred grand so he could save me from my own family. *(Laughing.)* Never trust a lady in a dingy.

(**DON GERONTE** *bolts up in outrage.*)

DON GERONTE. What? I'll –

FEATHER. I SAID CHANNEL SOME DAMN BUTTERFLIES.

DON GERONTE. Please stop yelling at me.

FEATHER. I'm defibrillating your aura, man, you need some hard medicine.

(**DON JERRY** *sits.*)

DON GERONTE. Maybe you should –

FEATHER. Ah ah. No advice from you, beat up homeless guy. I'm a grown-up person. I will solve my own problems. Jeeze, why can't you have a conversation with a man who doesn't have an opinion to share. You... Leo... Scapino...

DON GERONTE. *(Scowling.)* Scapino...

FEATHER. You know him?

DON GERONTE. Nope.

FEATHER. Then why did you say his name like that?

DON GERONTE. Like what?

FEATHER. *(Scowling.)* Scapino...

DON GERONTE. *(Scowling.)* Scapino... No reason.

FEATHER. Ugh, he's got his fingers in everybody's pies. He set his idiot lackey Sylvester to watch over me, and now he's planning some awful revenge on my tightwad potential future father-in-law for some slight he can't let go of. Should I be okay with that? I feel conflicted.

DON GERONTE. Oh, I thrive on conflict. And what is this tightwad skinflint cheapskate father-in-law's name?

FEATHER. Gillette? Germane? Jelly?

DON GERONTE. GERONTE?

FEATHER. Yeah, that's it. You know him? He sounds like a real idiot. After what Scapino pulled, I'm sure the whole town is laughing at him by now.

DON GERONTE. Oh yeah? Jerry Geronte may have the last laugh yet.

FEATHER. Maybe if this Jelly –

DON GERONTE. Jerry.

FEATHER. Maybe if this Jerry was more interested in the difference he could make instead of who he "was" people wouldn't be so eager to laugh at seeing him get screwed over. Hard to get humiliated when you live with a little humility. But what do I know? All right, I have to hide or run away or something. Well, beat up homeless guy? Feel better? I know it was a short session but what do you think?

DON GERONTE. *(Like a gathering then breaking storm of vitriol.)* Let me tell you what I think, miss hippie-dippie. I think the boy who told you he loves you is gonna get what's coming to him, and what's coming to him is not just a rotten apple like you. He's got *soooo* much more he's gonna answer for when his pop gets ahold of him. And Scapino? Who is patting himself on the backside for being so very smart? I'm thinking he is going to endure a reckoning that will make him sob and cry for his momma in a way he has not done since he was a tiny little conniving, swindling Scapino-baby. It will not help him. Because if I know this wiseguy, Don Jerry Geronte, and believe me, peacenik princess, I very much do know him…there is nothing on God's green beloved ever-loving Earth that will stop Don Jerry from drawing out Scapino's misery very slowly and with great satisfaction, in a deliciously creative, brutal, and unpleasant way. And just when the sweet release of death seems close enough that a brutalized and broken Scapino can almost taste it, he will watch his family, his neighbors, his pets, even the smiling barista at his favorite Starbucks pay the ultimate price for his oh-so-clever shenanigans. And only then, when he has lost everybody and everything, will this Scapino be shuffled off this mortal coil in the most hideous and stomach-churning way imaginable. But even *that* won't be the end... I am positive and without any doubt that Don Jerry Geronte will ensure the *name* Scapino will be scoured from this very earth and that his nameless ghost will wander aimlessly without a home, solace, or peace for all of eternity. And I think you can take that healing crystal and shove it up your chakras!

(He exits.)

FEATHER. What a douchebag.

Scene Four

*(SYLVESTER *runs in.*)*

SYLVESTER. Oh my God! There you are. Oh my God oh my God oh my God! Why did you leave the safe house?! And what the heck were you doing talking to Don Jerry?

FEATHER. Oh! So that's Don Jerry! No wonder he got so mad when I told him about Scapino.

SYLVESTER. You told him WHAT?

FEATHER. Oh, calm down, Sylvester, I didn't even mention you.

SYLVESTER. Oh, thank God.

FEATHER. Wait, oops, I did mention you.

SYLVESTER. OH MY GOD!

FEATHER. I was just carrying so much inside. It was such a burden. I had to let it out.

SYLVESTER. He's a maniac! It's curtains for me, Feather. Curtains!

FEATHER. He would have found out from someone else anyway.

SYLVESTER. I have to warn Scapino!

DON ALBERT. *(Offstage.)* Sylvester!

FEATHER. All right, just breathe, Sylvester. It'll all turn out okay in the end – this is a comedy. I'm gonna go find Leo and let him know what's going on.

Scene Five

(They start to exit in opposite directions, and **SYLVESTER** *runs into* **DON ALBERT.** **FEATHER** *clocks this and runs off.)*

SYLVESTER. Dead. Doomed...

DON ALBERT. Sylvester. Just the person I was looking for.

SYLVESTER. Yes sir.

DON ALBERT. I just ran into a pal of mine, Don Jerry Geronte. He told me the most fascinating story. I wanted to hear it from your own mouth. C'mon. Let's go for a little walk.

(DON ALBERT *and* **SYLVESTER** *start to exit.)*

Scene Six

(**DON GERONTE** *enters.*)

DON GERONTE. Where is he, you palmetto bug? You better start talkin' while you still have lungs to breathe.

SYLVESTER. I don't know Don Jerry! I swear! It was all Scapino's idea. I have been beguiled by his lawyerly charms!

DON ALBERT. That bastard screwed me out of fifty grand.

DON GERONTE. You got off easy. He screwed me for 100.

DON ALBERT & DON GERONTE. When I find him he's a dead man.

(*Beat.*)

DON ALBERT. Well, if nothing else he has mended the rift between us and united the families to one common purpose.

DON GERONTE. If only that could cheer me up, Don Albert. I just got word from my boys in Boca. My lovely wife, whom I had hidden there to protect her from the dangers of my lucrative, yet dangerous lifestyle...my boys tell me that my lovely wife has joined the angels in Heaven...natural causes. But my little girl, the little olive in my martini, my boys searched high and low for her but they tell me she's gone missing. They said she was last seen in the company of some wiseguy. I fear the worst. I...

(*He tries to hold it together but starts to cry.*)

DON ALBERT. Let it out, my friend. You have my deepest condolences. This tragic turn of events reminds me of my own daughter...my little princess Petunia who I lost to the angry seas so many years ago. She...

(*He starts to cry as he consoles* **DON GERONTE**. **SYLVESTER** *is moved by all of the emotion and starts to cry as well.*)

Scene Seven

(**CHLOE** *enters and sees them. Their sadness moves her and she starts to cry. After a time, the men notice her.*)

(*Everything stops.*)

DON GERONTE. ...Chloe?

CHLOE. ...Papa?

DON ALBERT. Papa?

DON GERONTE. Chloe!

CHLOE. Papa!

DON ALBERT & SYLVESTER. Papa!

(**DON GERONTE** *and* **CHLOE** *embrace. They all start crying again.*)

OCTAVIO. (*Offstage.*) Pop? Where are you, Pop?

DON ALBERT. All right, pull it together.

(*They all start to pull it together.*)

Here comes my son.

CHLOE. Here comes my husband.

(*Beat.*)

Your son?

DON ALBERT. Your husband?

DON GERONTE. You're married to his son?

DON ALBERT. You're married to my Octavio?

CHLOE. I am...

(*To* **DON ALBERT.**) Wait. You're my father-in-law?

DON ALBERT. Wait. That means –

DON ALBERT, CHLOE, DON GERONTE & SYLVESTER. (*Light bulb.*) Ohhhhhhhhhh...

Scene Eight

*(**DON GERONTE** and **DON ALBERT** share a look as **OCTAVIO** runs in.)*

OCTAVIO. All right, Pop, that's IT! This is me being a MAN, Pop. These boyish good looks are now mannish good looks. Oh man, Chloe, have you been crying? I... *(To his trousers.)* Down boy. *(To **DON ALBERT**.)* Pop, I'm in love with Chloe and we're married and that's that.

DON ALBERT. Octavio, I know, but what you don't know is...

OCTAVIO. I know everything I need to know, got it?

DON GERONTE. But she's my...

OCTAVIO. Look, with respect Don Jerry, I'm sure your daughter is a very nice girl but I am in love with Chloe.

DON ALBERT. Yeah, but she's...

OCTAVIO. I don't want to hear it, Pop. You see how firmly this chiseled jaw is set? That means I'm not gonna budge on this.

SYLVESTER. For God's sake, Octavio...

OCTAVIO. You too, Sylvester? I'll get you for this betrayal.

SYLVESTER. Oh my God, again?

DON ALBERT. Listen, Octavio, your wife –

OCTAVIO. Don't you dare besmirch the word "wife" unless it is smirched with my angel-face, Chloe. If you can't handle it, Pop, then here I am. I know what's in your pocket. Do your worst. Kill me here and now!

CHLOE. OCTAVIO! No! Live, Octavio! Jerry Geronte is my father! We've been reunited by almost unbelievable circumstances! I'm the mystery daughter you were destined to marry.

OCTAVIO. Wait. What? Woah. Really? You didn't know your pop was Don Jerry Geronte?

CHLOE. Yes! I mean no. I mean, my mom always told me he was in mergers and acquisitions...or was it murders and acquisitions?

DON ALBERT. Nice going, Octavio. You did good.

DON GERONTE. Yeah, what a blessing. I welcome you to the family.

CHLOE. And the way you stood up to your own pop? The danger you thought you faced that really didn't mean anything at all and just made you look like you didn't know what you were talking about? That was so hot.

OCTAVIO. Yeah?

CHLOE. Holy moly, yeah. Oh, Octavio.

OCTAVIO. Oh, Chloe.

(They start to go at it.)

DON GERONTE. All right, all right. No, no, no. What a happy day this is. Now I just need to punish my good-for-nothing son and kill Scapino and it'll be perfect.

Scene Nine

>(**LEO** *runs in.*)

LEO. Hey Pop.

DON GERONTE. Well, well, well. The prodigal son returns… for a beating he will never forget. Get over here.

LEO. No Pop.

CHLOE, OCTAVIO, DON ALBERT & SYLVESTER. *(Oh no he didn't.)* Oooooooooooo…

DON GERONTE. Did you just say no to me?

LEO. I did Pop. And you're not gonna like what else I have to say.

DON GERONTE. That's nothing new. Now listen up…

LEO. No, you listen, Pop. It's important…

>(**FEATHER** *runs in unnoticed while* **LEO** *steels himself. It spills out like a run-on sentence.*)

I met a girl who *saw into me*, Pop. Who challenged everything I ever thought about myself – and her smarts and smile and the smell of her patchouli sentenced the old Leo to death. My heart got a lethal injection, Pop. Old Leo is dead and I feel fresh and new – like a newborn baby-man. I've been reborn like a phoenix… CAW CAW! And if you can't accept that then I'm out. I'm leaving the family. I'm walking away.

DON GERONTE. You're walking a-*what*?…

FEATHER. Leo! You stood up to him. You really do love me.

DON GERONTE. What's twinkles the forest fairy doing here?

LEO. This is the girl I'm in love with, Pop! I want you to meet…

DON GERONTE. No… Leo, no! Anyone but that!

FEATHER. That's right, Jerry.

DON GERONTE. Never!

FEATHER. Wow! You need therapy, Grandpa.

CHLOE, OCTAVIO, LEO, DON ALBERT & SYLVESTER. *(Oh no she didn't.)* Tsssssssssssss…

DON GERONTE. Grandpa?! I still got it!

FEATHER. Not without a little blue pill, man.

CHLOE, OCTAVIO, LEO, DON ALBERT & SYLVESTER. *(Oh yes she did.)* Woah!

DON GERONTE. Why, I'll...

LEO. Pop!

DON GERONTE. Nobody walks away from Don Jerry Geronte.

LEO. Insult and smack me around all you want, kill me even, but I love this girl... *(Correcting himself.)* This person here. Nothing you can say or do will keep me from loving my Feather.

DON GERONTE. Loving your what?

OCTAVIO, CHLOE, LEO & SYLVESTER. Feather!

LEO. Her name is Feather.

FEATHER. It's short for Indigo Featherwest – the name my family gave me when they found me on the beach after a freak storm in the Gulf and saved me. They used to drive down here in their VW van when winters got too rough in Woodstock and camp out on the beach. They found me alone and crying in a dingy amidst a beach-wrecked boat named the Indigo Ocean.

DON ALBERT. Did you just say the Indigo Ocean?

FEATHER. Yeah, I did. What's it to you?

DON ALBERT. Feather, the Indigo Ocean was my family's yacht – it was my first wife's favorite pastime to drift in the Gulf for hours at a time and toss raw meat to the sharks that frolicked there. I found a hemp bracelet at the sight of the shipwrecked Indigo Ocean. A hemp bracelet but no daughter. I thought it was a hoop of seaweed.

CHLOE. Oh my God!

> *(She thrusts her arm in the air to show she's wearing a hemp bracelet.)*

> *(***DON ALBERT, DON GERONTE, LEO, FEATHER, OCTAVIO,*** and ***SYLVESTER*** gasp.)*

DON ALBERT. That hemp bracelet? Where did you get it?

CHLOE. Feather gave it to me. Isn't it rustic?

FEATHER. My family makes them.

DON ALBERT. *(Tentatively.)* Princess Petunia?

FEATHER. Daddy? Daddy!

(**FEATHER** *and* **DON ALBERT** *embrace.*)

DON ALBERT. My little girl. My little Feather has floated home.

OCTAVIO, CHLOE, FEATHER, LEO & SYLVESTER. *(Warmly.)* Awwww...

DON GERONTE. Wait. Feather is your daughter?

DON ALBERT. I know it seems unbelievable. Ludicrously so, but –

OCTAVIO. Yo! I got a big sister!

FEATHER. And I have a family again!

DON GERONTE. Just perfect.

FEATHER. That's right, Jerry. Like father like daughter. Who else in this town isn't afraid to stand up to your crap?

DON GERONTE. All right, that's it...

LEO. Pop, please. Don't turn this happy reunion into a bitter parting. Forgive me. And forgive Feather. For the family.

DON ALBERT. Yeah, Don Jerry. Let bygones be bygones.

CHLOE. Please, Papa.

LEO. Papa?

CHLOE. I'm your long-lost sister, Leo, try and keep up.

LEO. Oh. Does everybody know this?

DON ALBERT / DON GERONTE / OCTAVIO / CHLOE / FEATHER / SYLVESTER. Yes. / I knew it. / Well, yeah. / I just told you. / I just figured it out. / I have no idea what's going on.

LEO. Well ain't that a thing.

CHLOE. Pretty please, Papa? Feather and I have bonded! Look at my bracelet.

DON GERONTE. *(To **LEO**.)* You, I forgive always, eventually. Her, well, that healing mumbo-jumbo *did* work a little. But maybe that was just my natural positivity. All right, I forgive you. I must be getting soft. Welcome to the family.

DON ALBERT, CHLOE, FEATHER, OCTAVIO, LEO & SYLVESTER. *(Cheering.)* HEYYYYY!

FEATHER. And I forgive *you*, Gerald. You're just the radicalized victim of a male-dominated history that embraces the brutality of its leaders.

LEO. *(Overwhelmed and smitten by* **FEATHER***'s insight.)* SKABOOM!

FEATHER. We'll talk about it.

DON GERONTE. I can hardly wait.

FEATHER. Me neither. All right, Leo, where's the ring? You gonna get down on your knees and ask me to be your partner or what?

LEO. Oh! Wow. This is all happening so fast. I'm all a flutter. Ring? I…

FEATHER. Oh, what the hell.

> *(She gets down on a knee and slips a hemp bracelet on* **LEO***'s arm.)*

Leo, will you join me in a nontraditional ceremony and become my life partner? Say yes or you're dead to me.

LEO. Yes!

FEATHER. Great! Let's do it.

> *(***LEO*** and* **FEATHER** *kiss.)*

CHLOE, OCTAVIO, DON ALBERT, SYLVESTER & DON GERONTE. *(Warmly.)* Awwww…

LEO. Aw, Feather, I'm a phoenix. CAW CAW!

DON ALBERT. Don Geronte, welcome to the family. Let's share the spoils.

DON GERONTE. Yeah, let's. My turf is your turf. Fifty-fiftyish.

DON ALBERT. What a surprising and rewarding seven minutes this has turned out to be. You crazy kids. Come on, let's go to my place. Since you're all getting hitched I want to arrange a proper send-off.

DON GERONTE. Oh no, Don Albert. Tonight, I'm the one who's gonna spring for the biggest party our families have ever seen. You kids will tie the knot in style.

*(They all cheer and run off, except **DON GERONTE**, who intercepts **SYLVESTER**'s attempted exit with a brandished gun.)*

You? You are not family.

(Blackout.)

Scene Ten

(It is evening. **SCAPINO** *and* **SYLVESTER** *enter.)*

SYLVESTER. You better figure something out, Scapino! Fathers and sons, and daughters and fathers, and in-laws and outlaws, they've all reconciled. You can't play one against the other anymore. I knew we should have gone to Chicago as soon as we got the money. But oh no! You had to whack the hornet's nest even after you hoodwinked them out of their honey!

SCAPINO. Bees make honey, Sylvester. You're mixing metaphors again.

SYLVESTER. I don't even know what that means! I'm a limp noodle remember? Consequences schmonsequences. Remember that? Here we are, smack dab in the middle of schmonsequences. Don Jerry told me that unless I brought you to him by nightfall he was going to have his boys hunt me down like a twitchy little rabbit and there was no hidey-hole I could hide in that he wouldn't find.

SCAPINO. All right, we're going to Chicago.

SYLVESTER. He said he's got a lot of friends in Chicago.

SCAPINO. How does he know about Chicago?

SYLVESTER. I think it might have slipped out while he had a gun aimed at my face and I was crying like a baby and begging for my life.

SCAPINO. That'll do it.

SYLVESTER. How did I get into this mess? I'm too sensitive for this! I don't want to die in some horrible way! I want to die peacefully in my bed, an old man, surrounded by a loving wife and a little Sylvester Junior and an adorable fluffy kitty named Boo-Boo-Rumples-Flaburgenfeld. That's her Jellicle name. But not this way!

SCAPINO. Have a little faith! The deck may be stacked against us but we're still holding a straight flush.

SYLVESTER. A straight flush? Oh clever, how's this for clever?! Don Jerry's about to play "Go Fish!" by dumping our bodies in the Gulf of Mexico! Stop being such a smarty-pants and get us out of this! It's all falling apart!

SCAPINO. Sylvester...don't you dare fold. I got this.

SYLVESTER. Oh, nertz! Here they come. We should...wait! Where are you going?

(**SCAPINO** *and* **SYLVESTER** *exit hastily.*)

Scene Eleven

(**DON ALBERT**, **DON GERONTE**, **OCTAVIO**, **LEO**, **FEATHER**, *and* **CHLOE** *are all decked out for a wedding. There is a wedding dance lazzi showcasing all of them. The dance ends.*)

OCTAVIO. (*To* **DON ALBERT** *and* **DON GERONTE**.) Great party, Pops One and Pops Two. I look amazing.

LEO. Yeah, Pops. This is the bee's knees.

FEATHER. I don't ever want it to stop.

CHLOE. Octavio? Why have we stopped dancing! I want to see some moves!

OCTAVIO. Chloe, you ain't seen nothin' yet.

CHLOE. Not yet, I haven't. But the night is young!

(**OCTAVIO**, **CHLOE**, **FEATHER**, *and* **LEO** *slow-dance while* **DON ALBERT** *and* **DON GERONTE** *talk.*)

DON ALBERT. Ah, Don Jerry, tonight will be a night to remember! If only our lovely wives were still here to celebrate with us. I think it would have made them very, very happy. I think…

(*There is a brief moment of melancholy.*)

Well, let's make the evening a festive one.

Our families are reunited, our children are home. There is laughing. There is dancing. The music is playing. What could be more beautiful?

DON GERONTE. I could do with a little more Sinatra.

DON ALBERT. Who couldn't, Don Jerry. But that's our music, not theirs. They're the future, Don Jerry, and I think it's about time to pass the blowtorch. Ladies and gents, let's go inside and break open our finest barrel of hooch. I want to propose a toast to our new family. Stronger than ever!

(*They all cheer.* **SYLVESTER** *enters in despair.*)

SYLVESTER. Oh no! It's terrible...awful. Don Albert! Don Jerry!

DON GERONTE. Sylvester! Did I not tell you to bring Scapino to me or I'd...

SYLVESTER. That's what I'm trying to tell you! Scapino – He was on his way here to make amends. To throw himself at your mercy! The Scaramouches!

> (*He exits, then re-enters supporting a wounded* **SCAPINO.**)

The Scaramouche brothers made a hit, Don Jerry!

> (**SCAPINO** *is in terrible shape. Beaten...bloody... bandaged. Maybe shot a couple of times. Just terrible.*)

CHLOE. He looks pretty bad.

DON ALBERT. It looks like he wants to talk.

SCAPINO. Oh my friends...look at me. I'm done for. But I don't... (*Winces in pain.*) I've done some terrible and hilarious things, but now that it's curtains and the jig is up I want to greet St. Peter at those pearly gates like a man with a clear conscience. Please forgive me... especially you, Don Albert, and you, Don Jerry. You two whom I've hurt most of all.

DON ALBERT. I forgive you Scapino. May your soul rest in peace.

SCAPINO. Bless you, Don Albert. You're a gentleman. And you, Don Jerry. Is that a gun in your pocket or are you happy to –

DON GERONTE. It's a gun in my pocket.

SCAPINO. Oh, Don Jerry. It's you whom I've disrespected most of all. I put you in a sack. I beat you mercilessly...

DON GERONTE. I don't wanna talk about it.

SCAPINO. Please forgive me for beating you over and over...

DON GERONTE. All right, just shut up.

SCAPINO. Again and again.

DON GERONTE. Please shut up.

SCAPINO. Such a heavy stick...

DON GERONTE. Listen. Shut. Up. I forgive you everything already. Just stop talking.

SCAPINO. Forgiven. I can't believe it. So kind...so kind...

> *(He drifts away for a bit, mumbling to himself, then collapses.)*

LEO. This is pretty terrible.

OCTAVIO. Poor Scapino. A real bummer.

> *(There is a moment of silence.)*

DON ALBERT. All right. I'm going in.

SCAPINO. Goodbye, Don Albert.

DON ALBERT. Goodbye, Scapino. Flights of angels and all that...

SCAPINO. Goodbye, Don Jerry.

DON GERONTE. I forgive you on one condition...

FEATHER. Oh, lighten up, Jerry.

SCAPINO. And what condition is that?

DON GERONTE. You have to die.

SCAPINO. What?

DON GERONTE. Here. Now. If you get better, I take it all back.

SCAPINO. But...

DON GERONTE. *(Deadly serious.)* All of it. So go ahead. Any time. DIE, Scapino. I'll watch. I got time.

> *(They face each other, eyes locked. Then **SCAPINO** quietly looks to the rest of the family for help; they shrug with sympathetic detachment. **DON ALBERT** gestures that he should probably go ahead and get on with it. **SCAPINO** then looks to **SYLVESTER**, who is helpless and hopeless. Out of tricks and resigned to his fate, **SCAPINO** dies. Simply or histrionically, up to you. However that*

unfolds, when he does, there is a moment of silence. **FEATHER** *puts a hemp bracelet on* **SCAPINO***'s limp arm.* **CHLOE** *covers his eyes with a tissue.)*

I forgive you.

(The stage erupts into a wild, celebratory wedding dance, with the young lovers and **DON ALBERT** *dancing off to party the evening away.* **DON GERONTE** *does a victory dance over and around* **SCAPINO**, *then dances off to celebrate also.)*

*(***SYLVESTER** *is left alone onstage with the body of* **SCAPINO**.*)*

SYLVESTER. I told you this would happen, Scapino. Now how will I get to Chicago?

(He walks off in despair. A long beat. **SCAPINO** *sits up. He takes the time to undo his bandages and begins wiping the makeup off his face. He stands and begins to exit, but comes back downstage as he notices the audience. He gives them a wink and smile.)*

SCAPINO. ...Anybody need a lawyer?

(Blackout.)

End of Play